THE FALCON

THE FALCON

Shedrick B. Seton

VILLAGE TALES PUBLISHING

A catalog record for this book is available from the Library of Congress:
LCCN: 2016941728
ISBN: 9781945408045
eISBN: 9781945408052

Published By:
Village Tales Publishing
Lawrenceville, GA

Cover Design By:
OASS

www.villagetalespublishing.com
www.oass.villagetalespublishing.com

Printed in the United States of America

DEDICATION

Dedicated to the memories of
Maxwell Snotee, Prat Wleh
and Mother Patricia Jeffrey Chea.

For Anita, Shanita, Silvia and Sharon.

ACKNOWLEDGEMENT

I thank the President's Young Professional for giving me the opportunity to serve my country.

Thank you, Ms. Ophelia S. Lewis, for the guidance, support, and mentorship.

INTRODUCTION

Mother Supreme created a world with hope and aspiration for man's existence, and designed a silver and golden Falcon to provide them the necessities for survival. The universe was after her likeness, but her love for Fricano and Liberia surpassed all nations. Fricano emerged as the pilot of this creation. However, the cosmos angered Sister Sudan, master of praises and meditation and overseer of lifespan and timeline. So she diverted with a plan and man was given choices... a Pandora box.

Now Mother Supreme's lens projected a world filled with greed, strive, hypocrisy, and chaos mingling, producing a vortex of immoralities. Evils hovered over Ancient Fricano and spread its wings to the Negro Republic of Liberia. Now the last hope, the silver and golden Falcon of Good Fortune in Mother Supremes' court, was being contested by Sister Sudan and her freedom fighters. Mother Supreme had no choice but to prematurely send the Falcon to earth. Ancient Fricano received it, but lost its chance because of bloodshed. Although Liberia is messy, she received the Falcon.

Greediness and unpatriotic characters began choking the Falcon. Nigeria and Mali wished to possess it and tried stealing it. However, because of The Falcon's love for Liberia, it refused to leave. Their skirmish produced deadly diseases, famine, and backwardness.

Not giving up, Mother Supreme met with the heroes of Africa

and they prepared a remedy for their ailment. They also developed a plan for strategic growth and development. Zulu Menya is sent to heal the nation and he presented the plan to the government. Would they accept it?

CHAPTER ONE

The quietness of the courtroom denotes divine connectivity. Everyone performing the standing ovulation as the king entered the hall, head was slightly bent while chanting in a strange language. The king chanted mournful magical words as he walked toward the middle of the hall. He stopped and nodded at a guest seating in the balcony, above the throne. Chief Zoe Zeobon signaled that the guest stand. He did. The king walked to the front, stood before the throne. Everyone fell to their knees and shouted in the Soninke language, 'long live the king!' The king sat, and four giant dogs wearing four inch thick gold and silver necklaces, surrounded his throne. Four bodyguards—two on each side—positioned themselves behind each dog, posed as if ready to throw their spears.

The beauty of the courtroom was seen through a piece of

brown carpet hanging behind the large chair called The Throne. A nicely designed long piece of carpet, pinned between the roof and wall, lined from the left of The Throne to the entrance of the great hall, then back to the right of The Throne. The decoration enhanced the beauty of the large cream-color pillars which held up the roof. Giant sized sculptures of gold hung on the walls. Famous arts, like the flaked axes, the drills and arrowheads, hoes and jabbed pottery from Sijilmasa, Murzuk, Wadan and Agade's, hung on the wall. A carving of their king was placed directly over where the two departments usually sit during assembly or feast. One guard made sure everyone, before sitting, bowed and prayed to the king's statue positioned directly at the gateways of the two wings.

In the middle of the great hall, was a golden fountain designed akin to a salmon sitting in a bowl, letting out water. This fountain separated the throne from the Advisors' Sections. A long piece of sheep fur extended from the main entrance to the fountain, dividing Princes from Sons of Princes, and leaving the court into left and right. Another piece of sheep fur lined from the left of the hall to the fountain and continued to the right of the hall, showing the complete separation of power and orderliness within his government. The Princes and Sons of Princes from the three branches of government—the Royal, the Judiciary and the People's—sat directly opposite him, while non-commissioned officers sat at the back of the Princess and Sons of Princes.

The king's chair was of brilliant craftsmanship; thirteen feet tall and its backrest overlapped hung over the entire chair as if to secure shade. The head of the king was carved on the back of the chair, and the sparkling marbles that were placed in the sockets of the carved head, rotated clockwise and counterclockwise whenever the chair was touched. From a distance, the carved head appeared alive. Both arms of the chair were made of pure gold. The chair legs were decorated with eye-catching colorful fabric. Beneath the front of the chair was a stool made of gold, weighing ten tons, one which the king rested his feet while sitting.

The King looked at his corps of Advisors sitting at his right and smiled. They bowed. These Advisors were dressed in beautiful lappas with mixed colors of blue, green, yellow, black and white, as the lappas were suspended over their shoulders. A symbol, showing a triangular with two daggers overlapping at their pointed ends in the middle of it, was printed in the front of the lappas. A handshake, slightly situated within the handles of the daggers, was the symbol of the Zoes, referring to The Almighty Tattoo. The Zoes are people considered to have wisdom and mystical power, the heart and soul of the administration. The king decreed that each member of the higher echelon is mandated to go through the rituals of The Almighty Tattoo performed by the Zoes.

The Advisors were dressed in sleeveless shirts showing their tattoos, beads around their necks and ankles, and each holding a golden rod in his right hand. These Advisors were made of all fathers of the revolution, including relatives and family members of the core founders and strategists of the king's plan for occupation, of this resource-rich town.

He turned to his left and faintly smiled at officials of various departments. They, too, bowed. Each official wore a lappa with a falcon painted on it, and each one had three silver sticks in his left hands. King Koinyah stretched out his right hand toward the door behind the throne and, Youjay, the queen, took her seat on the chair next to him. Then he pointed at the entrance, and the drum called, Deba, sounded. The door keeper at the main entrance to the hall closed the door.

The king clapped his hands, the courtroom grew quiet, as a mournful atmosphere covered the room. King Koinyah stood and walked to the fountain to wash his hands, demonstrating his impartiality. The washing of his hands was also a ritual that signaled the commencement of the ceremony called, Convest. This end-of-year ceremony enabled the general department head and head of the princes and advisor, Huntoe, to report all projects completed during the year. Thereafter, the advisors would debate proposed projects meant for the following year. This particular year Convest ceremony was special and important; it coincided with the second twenty-year celebration of The Falcon. So the usual trends, like reporting to the body and festivity, were avoided. The Falcon was to prophesy the future of the kingdom.

King Koinyah clapped his hand three times and nodded. A door opened to a group of semi-naked girls dancing in pairs as they entered the courtroom. They entertained the courtroom for forty minutes, then danced their way out from where they had entered. Then Huntoe, Chief of Princes, stood. He walked to the throne and bowed. King Koinyah signaled him to stand erect.

"O King, Your Majesty," Huntoe declared, "Fricano, known to traders as 'The Land of Gold' has grown in territory. Its lands have been extended to the north and south of the Sahara. Our gold producing areas are packed with traders from across the sea. Our forty thousand Zenkepa trained warriors, armed with bow and arrows, shields, and iron pointed spears, proved our supremacy over our neighbors. Your acquisition of ten thousand camels, and fifty thousand well bred dogs of war, are evident of your plans for the building of a great civilization. Our kingdom is also known as a mighty empire throughout the world because of our relationship with Zenkepa. The embassy of Zenkepa in Fricano is the biggest in this region, and the intermittent visit of advisors and businessmen from Zenkepa shows the strength of our economy. My Lord, the Ruler of the earth, your kingdom will reign forever."

Huntoe finished, bowed and took his seat.

King Koinyah nodded to Huntoe's praises.

As Huntoe sat, the clinking noise of an opening door sounded from the far right wing of the hall. An old man, with gray beard nearly touching the ground, entered the courtroom. His long gown, designed to follow him, dragged carelessly behind. The old man moved fluidly as he walked to the throne. He bowed, then turned to face the entrance. He recited something in a mixed repetitive tone while waving his right hand. A whirl of thin smoke suddenly appeared. The old man chanted again, this time, using magic words. This created a square-looking opening in the sheep fur two meters away from him, and just six meters from the throne.

Bewilderment tangled all. Everyone grew quiet.

Smoke scurried out of the hole and immediately cleared away. Then the voices of people singing followed, coming from the deep inner layer of the earth. The singing suddenly changed to an increased pitch of praise and worship shouts. Afterward, light cast by rays, and flaming balls, shot out of the earth like fireworks. At that instant, the head of a falcon ascended slowly in ice fog smoke. And when it reached its desired height, balls of blue light sprung out of its body.

The old man quickly waved his magical wave, whirling the light balls toward the king. The King twisted and turned in his seat. He began screaming and grinding his teeth as these balls entered his body, shocking him. Moments later, a light cloud surrounded his body as he calmed down, sitting in what looked to be the haze of a comet. Red-eye, King Koinyah held on tightly to the armrests, shaking with laughter as if possessed. As the light balls of vitality and strength settled into him, he slowly regained his composure.

The Falcon came to rest on a golden plate, five-inches thick. A light cast by rays dangled over its head and disappeared. The Falcon had gold and silver portions; twenty-five-inch thick gold, and eighteen-inch thick silver. The seven-foot square-sloping stool on which it sat, was also made of pure gold.

Then, two giant men walked in, each carrying a virgin (a boy and a girl) toward The Falcon and the old man. They reached the front, holding the frightened children firmly in their grip. The old man prepared his knife and the children stiffened. He chanted as he worked his knife easily, or rather quickly, through their necks, one after the other. Knowledgeable in their role, the giants turned the children's bodies upside down, holding them by their legs, allowing blood to flow onto The Falcon. Few inches on the silver portion on the falcon turned to gold. A slight firework explosion encircled it, showing that the gods were satisfied with the sacrifice. The old man chanted once more, and The Falcon lifted itself and slowly descended into the earth's crust. The opening, from which it had come, sealed on its own.

The old man started to take his place when the door to the main entrance opened. It had been forced open.

"Hold it! Hold it!" a man dressed in rags, shouted. He was pointing at the king. "You, evil incarnate! Your administration has reduced the people to mere beggars. Their daughters are the juice to quench the sexual burning thirst within you, and your men. You took my son's wife and made her yours. The gods will never forgive you for such devilish arts… she will never give you children."

Everyone sat mute.

"Knowledge has been dispersed, and the swords appreciated," the man in rags continued. "Pampamyou, the highest institute of spiritual learning, has lost its credibility. It is now a place where your thugs disrupt normal learning activities. You must know that knowledge brings understanding, and understanding places one in the highest orders of mystical achievement... and tolerance...."

Two bodyguards moved towards him. The speaker moved backwards, pulling two daggers from his side. He pointed them at the bodyguards.

"Chief Kolluba had the vision to create a paradise of hope," the man in rags continued. "A land of liberty, but your passion for the swords have blinded your sight and understanding. Don't you know that the people are the kingdom and the kingdom, the people? A circle? Treat them well and live in peace... treat them bad and live in fear.

"Remember, a country that was surrounded by people and swords; the King's interest was only in the sword. He was using the sword, according to him, to correct his subjects. The people could not speak of the goodness of their King anymore. They fasted and prayed that their gods would rescue them. One of his ministers knew the power of the people and openly challenged the King's method of correcting the people. He was sentenced to death. The people rebelled, accusing the King of wanting to kill the liberator, and that was his end.

"You will not complete the cementing of The Falcon with gold," he went on. "The people in the north no longer rejoice in your name. Your name has become continental evil! Your so-called systems of government are drawn like this: the king of the Royal Branch is seen sitting on the Judiciary Branch, which has

15

been infested with members of the Zoes. You are all using the People Branch as your footstool. My son will rise up an army that will bring your reign to an end. Now, order your dogs to do me like you've done to the others, the people's mouth," the ragged man finished and dropped his daggers.

He remained standing. Smiling.

"Who is that… thing?" the King shouted angrily. "I do not want to see him again! Ever!"

The bodyguards forcefully took hold of the ragged man, then dragged him out.

Huntoe got permission to speak.

"My King, he is called, Korluba," Huntoe said, "a local magician who failed miserably on the test to enter Zenkepa… a foster father to the renegade, Kpa Por… a nobody."

King Koinyah's nostrils flared, the vein in his neck became engorged.

"But my Lord," Huntoe continued, "you and this kingdom can never fall. The Falcon has empowered you for thirty more years. In fact, the people talk freely under your administration. Several persons are now jealous of your ingenuity in leading the people, so they are misusing this freedom to talk. But my Lord… my King, I believe it is time you protect us against the danger this freedom to talk is producing."

King Koinyah held his chin high.

"As you know, my Lord, jealousy contains a lot of alcohol; several persons don't have the willpower to withstand the intoxicating components. Their reactions will demonstrate the sound of angry ocean waves… the roar of a lion… the hissing of a poisonous snake, or the creeping of a cat. But my Lord, you are the greatest of all Kings on this continent… the source of gold. And, like the grandson of King Tunka Manin, the greatest warrior ever lived.

"Moreover, words are an empty vase if not given credence. You love your people and want them to follow orders for the general good of our kingdom. Fricano has grown in military strength and economic power because of your ability to lead with compassion and tolerance. My Lord, may you live forever," Huntoe finished and took his seat.

King Koinyah raised both hands and signaled that the festivity continue.

Liberation was certain.

Two special guards took hold of the ragged man, who's actually a soothsayer, by his legs. They hauled him into the forbidden forest where the smell of decayed human flesh greeted them upon entrance. The forest had served as a correction center for thugs, criminals, enemies of the kingdom, and traitors. On orders of the king, two separate structures were constructed for rehabilitation purposes; one for women and the other, for men.

The structure used for women has three units, a symbolic belief that a woman enters the world three times before her final death. The first room, about one hundred feet in length, is considered the period of development from childhood to womanhood. A convicted woman is stripped of her clothes and ordered to crawl in mud knee-deep until she reaches a second room. If she delays, the guards, walking on sticks, are instructed to beat her constantly until she reaches the end. When she reaches womanhood, she is vulnerable to be grabbed and raped by ten men. The woman has to bleed before she is allowed to enter the next room. If there is no blood, she is never allowed to pass. She will be raped repeatedly. Many women lost their lives in this room. However, if she survives long enough to reach the last room, she is tied to a log only to await the single stroke of an executioner's ax.

In the men's structure, the first unit is dark as night, and filled with flesh-eating ants. A prisoner's hands are bound at his back and his legs tied, before he is thrown into the ants' pit. He is expected to crawl on his belly to reach the next room, fatherhood, where he is castrated. Then, he is led to a second room, called wisdom, where his eyes are blinded using a red-hot iron. Then liquid-glue is poured into both ears, causing him to become deaf. This is done according to the belief that the sources of wisdom and understanding are the eyes and ears.

The last room is for eternal condemnation. The prisoner is stretched on a flat surface, his arms and legs tied to four poles, as he awaits the executioner's ax to divide him in two equal parts. The body is left as is, to decompose.

CHAPTER TWO

A loud noise echoed through the terminal as the DC-747 prepared to land. The plane landed, then taxied toward the terminal and stopped. As the doors were being opened, the overhead speakers announced to the arrivers in their official French language, then in English, "Welcome to Bamako Senou International Airport... welcome to Mali."

The passengers exited the plane, holding on to their carry-on, and then followed the sign to the immigration counters in a two-line formation. One line was for the French-speaking arrivers and the other, for English-speaking passengers.

"Hello, Madame," the immigration officer greeted the first passenger. "May I see your passport?"

She handed the officer her passport, he flapped through the

pages, selected what he wanted, stamped the page, then handed it back to her.

"Next!"

A man stepped up; six-foot-two with muscly torso to boot. He was wearing a three-piece navy blue suit, sky blue shirt, a crimson tie, and black Pierre Cardin shoes. His physique portrayed the likeness of Schwarzenegger during his bodybuilding days, except he was African.

"Your passport, sir," the immigration officer asked.

The gentleman handed him his passport, and he did as he had done with the woman's. The officer stared admiringly as he handed him back the passport. He nodded and took his passport. Then, he swang his carryover bag across his shoulder and headed for the exit doors.

"Bonjour Monsieur," a man greeted the gentleman as soon as he stepped out of the terminal.

"How do you do," the gentleman replied.

"I have a taxi, if you need one," the man said. "I can take you anywhere you wish."

"You do speak English."

"Yes. I am a Liberian, a refugee here. I am working for someone. So, may I help with your beg?"

"No, you may not," the gentleman replied.

"You can trust me, sir. My car, that Datsun station wagon across the street," he pointed, "is mine."

"I'll follow you there," the gentleman said, still holding on to his bag.

They walked to the station wagon and the gentleman boarded the front seat.

"Take me to the Comme Chez Soi Hotel, please."

THE FALCON

✳✳✳✳

The airport was about fifteen kilometers south of downtown Bamako. Bamako got its name from the Bambara word meaning, crocodile river. The city is located at the mouth of the River Niger, and the fertile lands of the river provided the people with an abundance of food supply. It is believed that the early kingdoms became wealthy from established trade routes linking across West Africa, the Sahara, and leading to northern Africa and Europe.

The November breeze was indeed cool and refreshing. The passenger rolled down his window, taking in the scenery of people busying themselves about their business. But nothing could take his mind of the dreams he had had for five consecutive days. In this dream, an old man poured olive oil over his head and presented him a silver and gold falcon. "This is your destiny," the old man told him. Every time he woke up and went back to sleep, the dream was the same.

"How long have you stayed in Mali," the passenger asked.

"Nine years," the driver replied. "My name is, Moses... Moses Snoteh."

"And, I'm "Nagbe Koffa," replied the gentleman.

"Oh, you are a Kru man," Moses exclaimed. "A Liberian!"

Then in the Kru language, Moses asked Nagbe about Liberia and his visit to Mali.

"This is a business trip, although it is to buy Arts," Nagbe replied. "I am the secretary to the deputy minister for cultural affairs at the Ministry of Tourism. I, along with seven others, was sent all over West Africa to buy famous arts for the museum."

"I know where you can get some valuable arts," Moses

informed. "The Golden Stool of the Ashante, for instance… and other valuable ones. They are reasonably priced too. We could use my car, or we can take a train to Timbuktu."

"I prefer your car," Nagbe suggested.

"It's set, then," Moses replied.

"Why don't you come by the hotel and pick me up," Nagbe said.

Moses drove over a bridge, made a right turn, then traveled a few more kilometers before coming to a stop in front of the Comme Chez Soi Hotel.

"So, tomorrow morning, then," Nagbe reminded, and handed Moses a twenty-dollar US bill, more than the actual cost.

Nagbe Koffa checked in at the front desk and soon after, ushered into his room on the third floor by a uniformed doorman. The man opened the door, and stepped aside. Nagbe walked in, tipped him; and as soon as the man walked away, he closed the door.

Tropical aroma filled the room, obviously with more smell of pineapple than anything else. It had a full-size bed with nightstand on both sides. Nagbe turned on the TV, and then headed to the bathroom to give it a thorough inspection. He pulled back the shower curtain, turned the faucet on, then off. He repeated this testing at the sink, and then flushed the toilet. All to his satisfaction, he returned to the bedroom and sat on the bed.

Nagbe turned the television station to CNN just as a beer commercial was ending. He reached for the phone and ordered burgers and orange juice to be brought to his room.

CNN news continued with a special reporting of the Zairian's war. This reminded Nagbe of the civil war in Liberia, and how things had progressed since. Monrovia, which had suffered the most during the war, was now a place of attraction. Major streets had both human and automobile traffic. Market stalls were packed and consumers filled their wants. The war had brought untold hardship to the people in the city and the rest of the country. While one faction burned down schools, others destroyed stores and people's homes. Outlaws looted, rebels killed civilians and people starved indiscriminately. Many drank dirty water to satisfy their thirst. Liberian youths had no hope for their future, their dreams were sinking as fast as people were dying.

Then the Economic Community of West African States Monitoring Group (ECOMOG), with the assistance of the United Nations, brought about peace. Elections were held, and the six-man transitional government was replaced with a democratic one. Later that year, the government announced the Reconstruction Tax law passed through the unicameral legislature, in which everyone earning an income would pay, besides his income tax, one third of his salary. This tax was applied to the government revenue for reconstruction.

There were other bills sent to the legislature; among them, a bill to change the name of the country, a bill to denounce Joseph Jenkins Roberts as Liberia's first president because he had been born in the United States. Another bill was to change the map of the country, placing Americo-Liberians in one half and Native-Liberians in a greater half. The official seal and flag were to be changed as well, citing the Coat of Arms showed oppression toward one group of Liberians. The mandate of yet another bill, required every citizen to either take a native name, or placed a native name amongst his actual name. Every Americo-Liberian was to pay reparations for taking over the land of their African fathers, and denying Native-Liberians the right to partake in business ventures or investing in the natural resources because they believed that Native-Liberians had not the capacity to handle such ventures that required professionalism and accountability.

Massive destruction brought on by the civil war had placed a great need of money for the government. The government, with more care for business than people, initiated a tax holiday for its investors. This was good for business; however, keyed principles to spur growth and human resource development were deserted. They left out policies that would discourage ethnic and social divides or strong laws against corruption. Not even self-reliance was given any thoughts. The government failed to include the means of acquiring funding for a national stature of healing, forgiveness and reconciliation; the suggestion of a five-hundred-foot pillar with a giant dove sitting at the top, holding a palm straw in its mouth. It was hoped, that every citizen who had lost a loved one would place a candle at the foot of the stature on Decoration Day, a holiday to remember those who had lost their lives.

The government made no genuine provision for the re-identification and maintenance of culture and tradition, nor did it reintroduce the suggested slogan, One People-One Nation-One Liberia, that would strengthen the quest for a national identity. Their policies only focused on rebuilding damaged infrastructures and investors flooded the country to explore and exploit.

It was at this time that the National Museum was identified and great importance was given for its replenishment. Eight Liberian Art Appraisals, including Nagbe Koffa, were selected to tour the world in search of famous art pieces.

The next morning, Nagbe was having his breakfast in his room when the phone rang. The receptionist informed him that Moses

Snoteh was there to pick him up. Nagbe joined Moses and soon they were on their way to Timbuktu.

CHAPTER THREE

A momentous silence covered the Castle of Grace early one morning as the Breeze traveled from Mother Supreme's bosom while she sat in the Hall of Meditation conducting the regular exhaling expirations. Every morning the Breeze travels from the Hall of Meditation and spreads throughout the earth, entering the nostrils of all mankind to rejuvenate the human souls. At exactly midnight, those marked for death or pardon, receives either death or the breath of hope from Mother Supreme's Cane of Fate. During this tour of duty, Take-Away and Brother Hope, when they had travelled in the same direction, expressed opinions about certain creations. There were also times when they traveled in opposite directions.

The Castle of Grace is meant for morning devotional activities, but Sister Sudan started an argument soon after the exhaling expirations, expressing her unsatisfaction of how Mother Supreme distributes innate abilities to mankind, as well as her unfair decisions on who lives or dies. The conduit between earth and the heavens, Sister Sudan was the master of praises and meditations.

The overseer of man's life span, Sister Sudan also supervised man's timeline and supported all laws of nature. However, Mother Supreme controlled all, and did; often creating some people with exceptional aptitude, connecting their souls directly to hers. These people she referred to as, 'those after my heart'. King David, destined to rule his people, was one of those after her heart, while King Saul was denounced—Sister Sudan's opinion. Sister Sudan loved King Saul, thus condemning Mother Supreme's partiality in administering the affairs of the lesser gods and mankind.

Then, one particular report angered Sister Sudan; Mother Supreme was to send The Falcon of Good Fortune to the earth, to a country to be named, Liberia. And, this undertaking she thought, would make man lazy.

"I will never stand and see you do that again," Sister Sudan snapped at Mother Supreme.

To which Mother Supreme replied, "Your duty is to praise and worship me, a duty of a lesser deity. Archangels don't question me… but, you… you want to challenge my authority."

"It is not a challenge, Mother Supreme," Sister Sudan replied. "The Hebrew's selection of Saul as their king, is contrary to your interest… and the distribution of innate talent among the lesser deities, as well as the rest of mankind, are driven by your interest. Why?"

"Now, you asked, 'why'?"

"Well, you created man like us, in appearance and behavior, possessing the same level of mystical maturity. You created King

David to be so brave, that he destroyed kingdoms. Then, King Menes of Egypt, more powerful than other kings… Alexander the Great, to have conquered places on the earth, and Hitler, yes, even Hitler, who challenged the world. You, Mother Supreme, you deliberately make things with opponents, and opposites, just to create chaos and destruction….”

“I decide how much power to give,” Mother Supreme interrupted. “And, how much rain to fall… the amount of sunshine to dry up the water… when it should be dark or when daylight comes. I am the omnipotence, the omniscience and I control the daily affairs of mankind!”

“It’s an illusion,” Sister Sudan challenged. “Isn’t it the law of motion that keeps everything in its place? A twist in the spiral line of the laws will always have an advert effect. Are you saying you will continue to direct the affairs of man whom you’ve created in your image and likeness?”

Mother Supreme gave no reply.

“I see why man cannot turn water into wine,” Sister Sudan continued. “But I can assure you, my two children, Arka and Zula, whose fates I will direct on earth, will teach man how to get wine out of plants. Arka will take my evil nature, while Zula will take my good nature. These two natures, when combined in a single mating, will produce a child that will share the power of both natures. However, the stronger will rule the mind and the earth will either be in peace or confusion.”

“Sister Sudan, I am the source of all what nature has to offer,” Mother Supreme reminded. “I suppress the wicked and clang on to the good. Man can do the same.”

“Confusion,” cried Sister Sudan.

“They will find a solution.”

"Even disunity?" Sister Sudan said, incredulously.

"They will build alliances, Sister Sudan," Mother Supreme replied.

"Alliances? How? My neighbor's son was sent into the world to have dominion over everything. He found himself in a family, a community, a nation. He had no dominion over anything because you made him to be at the bottom of the social ladder. He was dispersed because of the color of his skin... he had no money, and was of the tribe described as uncivilized. He never had control over himself... his spirit, we controlled. His body and mind? Controlled by environment and situation. What a dominion... and a fantasy? Don't you think it is a situation of injustice and unequal rights? Why would you babysit people of the earth who should be working harder, and reaping from what they sowed? You will not be appreciated if you make life so easy for this generation... manna falling from the sky to increase their social pleasures. And in so doing, their allegiance to you will shift to what they will feel comfortable praying to. I don't think you would like that."

"If you are playing politics, Sister Sudan, don't," Mother Supreme said. "What you said is treasonable. Is it not indirectly related to the Falcon of Good Fortune, which I am about to send to Africa? Especially a country to be established? Liberia? Liberia will be dashed and rejected by its founder."

Sister Sudan exploded into laughter. "You must be joking Mother Supreme," she went on. "Africa will move from slavery... to colonization, then to freedom fighters, and to identity crisis... and back to political, social and economic slavery, or colonization. Will disunity and uncertainty allow a Falcon of fortune to survive? The gospel of the Falcon will not change the status code, but it will be charged with blasphemy and hung. I will exchange it with a duplicate… a Falcon with the magical choice between hard work and getting things easily… sincerity and insincerity…. self-love and love for country… unity and disunity, greed and generosity.

"Africans will choose between the two, and that choice will lead them to their destiny. I will stand as a bridge between you and mankind, Mother Supreme, so that you may no longer come in direct contact with them. You have given me my share of power and I intent to use it to the fullest. I hope the rediscovered Africa will ably manage or get the best out of those vast resources. They will have abundant resources, you'll see, and others will plunder it. And, the gains from the spoil will lead to disunity and confusion."

"And, your name would be used for the massive extinction of people," Mother Supreme voiced angrily. "Those people would be used… drained… deranged… broken, and even destroyed."

"I will use my power to return them to the continent and my name will be restored," Sister Sudan said. "The question should be, will they forgive you? Will they love you? Will they appreciate you? Perhaps, they won't even remember you as their source of existence."

"Guard! Seize Sister Sudan and put her in the pit of rehabilitation and corrections," Mother Supreme ordered.

Before the guards could take hold of the Master of Praises and Meditations, she shouted, "Freedom fighters, attack," and vanished into thin air.

Four members of the Genge, Mother Supreme's special soldiers, entered the Hall of Grace and vanished in the spiritual realm, following Sister Sudan; while three Genge guards battled the Freedom Fighters. Two other Genge guards sort Mother Supreme's orders.

"We await your orders, Mother Supreme."

"Go, at once, to the island in the middle of River Lue," Mother Supreme ordered. "Protect the Falcon of Good Fortune."

In the main time, Sister Sudan and her freedom fighters were engaged in a grim battle with the Genge guards in the first spiritual realm called, Connuka.

The River Lue, located in the inner heavens, has its source under Mother Supreme's throne. There, twelve girls (each representing a month in the revolution of the earth) sat, singing a soulful melody. Their tears overflowed the River Lue and formed loops, causing rain to fall in different parts of the earth. This magnificent attraction of the earth, created by Mother Supreme, is a demonstration of the earth's motion by Pa Grafy, who sits with both his palms positioned around the globe, moving his hands back and forth, spinning earth towards the sun and then away from it. This force is called, Windosphere.

The Genge guards repelled Sister Sudan and the Freedom Fighters, thus capturing, and later, sending her into purgatory for a century or so.

The Falcon of Good Fortune, you see, was destined to enrich Africa, mainly Liberia, with minerals and crude oil. However, Sister Sudan yearned for the Falcon to be sent to the earth where a lot more people would benefit. She would rather people unveil the puzzle of life through search and work, rather than getting things free.

Centuries later, in the realm of rehabilitation and corrections, also called post-purgatory, an impious interlock of the three elements associated with passionate symphony of marvelous, touched. The luminosity of the conjugality of these elements— Earth, Water, and Fire—reflected the supreme craftsmanship of the collaborative inputs from the highest orders of creation. In the middle of the interlock, was a point of attraction which served as a booster to a web of tiny spiral lines, spinning in motion. From a distance, the point appeared like a tornado. The midpoint of the interlock, known as the Point of Identity, compromised the Past, Present and Future.

The Past narrated what was and never would be; a position of failure and regrets, or gains or contention. A moment of loss which struggles to catch up with time, but too slow and fragile for the strife. The Present was a shadow, susceptible to slip into the past, but with continuing motion in time. The radiance of Time slowly wears down its present reality; thus, unconsciously pushing the Present in the Past. And the Future is what shall be, or never will be. Time, it seems, is too slow for the Future, so it hangs on a flicker of the Present in hope of entering the Future.

Anyone coming out of the Point of Identity was certain to have digested the three Intrinsic Worths through which he decides his own fate. Once he has internalized the three Intrinsic Worths— Feminine, Masculine and Neutrally- willed—he is taken into Centum-infinite to observe interactions and mystical interplays. And then, he can specialize based on a particular interest. This process through post-purgatory is meant to set the state for entry into the world, a structural rebirth.

The first few months of a child, during the period of rebirth, is the Pace Setter. The years following are, the Period of Recollections and then, Interest. Interest will lead to the physical realization of interactions and interplays. From the interactions and interplays in purgatory, specialization in the real world will be driven by those three virtues; Feminine, Masculine and Neutral.

Sister Sudan had entered into purgatory; and her body, mind and spirit concomitantly traveled through Earth, Water and Fire.

She converged at the Point of Attraction. Her travel into Centum-infinite enabled her to witness the deliberation of Socrates, Aristotle, Machiavelli, Nietzsche, Hegel, Plato, Francis Bacon, Spinoza, Voltaire, Immanuel Kant, Adolph Hitler, Alexander the Great, Bin Laden, John Locke, Idi Amin, Rousseau, Napoleon, Koinyah, Karl Max, and other gifts of wonders and evil. She saw well governed kingdoms rising and falling in Africa.

She entered the library at Timbuktu. She formed Martin Luther King, Jr, Malcolm X, Marcus Garvey, Edward Wilmot Bladen, and others whom she believed would be poetic, scientific, and ingenious. She considered the discourses of Adolph, Ben, Nietzsche, Karl, the ambitions of Napoleon and Alexander, and others who would impact the world from their little pragmatic corners, a beast-pan. She found satisfaction in the Gospels of Jesus, Buddha, Martin Luther, Gandhi, and those who perceived the world as an egg, and especially those who believed in a world free of prejudice.

This rebirth of Sister Sudan fell into the grace of Mother Supreme, and Mother Supreme pardoned her. Mother Supreme, however, later sent the Falcon to the earth before the appointed time. She instructed the Father of Good Fortune, Zangula Ouita, to take the Falcon and deliver it to the village of his choice; a village, which he believed, to have the potential to elevate itself to a kingdom. Mother Supreme also permitted Sister Sudan to go along and be its principle guidance.

* * * *

One day, centuries later, the sun had reached its peak in

Bentue, a small village in the northwestern region of Africa, when winds from north of the Sahara made waves of desert sand. The wind, increasing with pressure, blew from all directions. Then, in a very short while, a dune of about fifty feet in height, erected meters from the village.

Cardify Nygue, chief of the village, stopped in his tracks. He had just returned from the oasis, calabash in hand, and filled with water. All of a sudden, a silver door at the base of the dome opened, and an old man walked out.

"Cardify," the old man greeted, and started toward him, "Good luck, and good day."

Cardify shuddered with fear. The calabash fell out of his hand, spilling its content. As fast as the water had spilled out, a wooded Falcon, silver and golden in color, appeared in the wet sand.

"I am, Zangula Ouita, Father of Good Fortune," the old man introduced himself. He reached out and touched Cardify's face, using his right hand. The continent of Africa instantly appeared in the chief's vision.

Cardify stood in awe of the rich tropical forest to the west and the gold and diamond fields in the south. There were more forests in the east. Then, his eyes followed the desert in the north of the continent. This scene passed, and Cardify saw people, Africans, dancing to the rhythm of drums. The people were rejoicing and singing, "Mother Supreme! Mother Supreme, we love you. We enjoy the milk you feed us from your breasts! O how we amuse ourselves in the jungle of your arms. Thank you, Mother Supreme, for giving birth to mankind. We cherish you always."

Children and adults sang and danced in circles.

Then, quick as a turning page, Cardify saw new people. They were not Africans, and they were different. In appearance, that is.

These people he saw were engaged in strange activities; they were catching African people. They beat them as they caught them. Then they put chains around their necks and marched them to large wooden vessels waiting on the sea. They did this to men and women, lads and maidens; old men, old women and even children. Small children. Those who rebelled, were whipped and, at times, killed.

But these African people continued to sing, and they sang a new song.

"Mama Supreme! Oh! Mama Supreme, how long will you stay away? Can't you see that we have been driven out of our homes? They are killing our prophets. Are you powerless, as we are? Are your arms too short to reach us? These people are using evil against us for our good. Why do you watch and do nothing?"

Suddenly, the earth quaked from the tip of Good Hope in the South, to Mount Kilimanjaro in the East; from the Atlas Mountain in the North, down to Mount Nimba in the West. Then, at the south of the continent, rays of light encircled it in colors of blue, yellow, green, red, black and white lines. Mother Supreme stretched forth her arms and gathered the children.

By now, these strange people had given sticks of every kind, to the African people. They had been taught to use these sticks against each other. Some even killed their own prophets. Sadly, this angered Mother Supreme and she let go of the African people. They scattered in numbers, great and small, across the continent; it seemed, never to unite again.

Cardify regained consciousness.

"You saw things," Zangula Ouita said, "strange things. Did you not?"

"I did, Oh, holy one," Cardify's voice quivered.

"Those things will come to pass," Zangula Oiuta told him. "It will happen in the great future. Mother Supreme has sent me to give you this Falcon. An empire will rise and you are to give this Falcon to the king. You will be its caretaker. The Falcon, I mean."

Zangula Quita handed Cardify the Falcon.

"The Falcon will gather resources through supernatural powers, to make this empire great," Zangula Quita, continued. "You are to bring the Falcon out every twenty years for a celebration. During the festival, the people must give Mother Supreme praise, and you will see the silver portion on the Falcon turn to gold. Mother Supreme expects everyone to enjoy what she gives. If the king performs the exercise two times in fifty years, what you witnessed will never happen. This place will be a place of sanctuary. However, if the king mislead the people and rejects what Mother Supreme has offered, great suffering will come upon the empire and the continent will suffer terribly."

Zangula Ouita finished and disappeared.

Cardify gained composure and ambled home, keeping the entire phenomenon to himself. Such incident would trouble anyone, and Cardify was no exception. He lay on his bed troubled, as sleep was long in coming. He twisted and turned for hours, yet sleep did not come. So, he remained awake, lying on his back, staring at the ceiling.

He did not know when it happened, or how it happened. But as he looked toward the ceiling, strange writing appeared. At first, Cardify did not recognize the writings, but as the letters disarranged, then rearranged in heteromorophic inscriptions, he knew its meaning: the holy one has come to visit you.

A tiny bright light grew out of the writing, and increased in size. Then, a woman's figure followed. The figure moved slowly until she landed at Cardify's bedside.

"Peace be unto you, Cardify," the figure voiced. "I am, Sister Sudan, spiritual head of one million generations. I control your generation, as well as your fate. Where is the Falcon?"

"The Falcon?" Cardify asked. "But, it was given to me."

"Of course, Cardify. But should you rebel against your creator or your guidance?"

"This is earth," Cardify retorted. "On earth, I'm master of my destiny."

"No, Cardify," Sister Sudan replied. "I, am your master in Connuka and on earth. Everything you do, is controlled by laws and I put those laws in place. Now, do you believe, your being on earth disassociates you from the network?"

Cardify gave no reply.

Sister Sudan sighed.

"The firmness and uniqueness of the laws give you justice," she continued. "What is due you? Do what is required of you on earth, and do what is required of Connuka. Connuka needs only worship and praises, soaked with thanksgiving. However, purify yourself before giving Connuka its share.

"You claimed to be master of your destiny," Sister Sudan said, incredulously. "Were you told that you are made in Mother Supreme's image and likeness? Ah, yes, Cardify, you are your own master. But, you see, lack of knowledge kills the strife. You do have substance, a physical vessel that hosts Mother Supreme's image and representation. This is true. But, do you expect Mother Supreme, or me, or any creation in Connuka, to farm for you? Do you expect us to perform on earth for you, those virtues of life that you are made of?"

Cardify gave no reply.

"You don't have to ask Connuka for guidance because it is already in you," Sister Sudan continued. "Search within yourself. Understand and conquer. Bring out the good found in nature to enhance your life. If King Menes question you, ask him for your happiness. If you fail in your duty and responsibilities, then ask Connuka for forgiveness."

Finally, Cardify spoke.

"Why are you telling me these things?" he asked.

"For your spiritual growth," Sister Sudan replied. "A son can question his father's position, but can you question the act of Connuka, or Mother Supreme? No," she replied before Cardify could.

"Life on earth, is for you to do for yourself… your family… your kinsmen and, for King Menes. Question his use of words and his deeds. If he strikes you, question him for your method of dying. Tell him how you want to die. Remember, life on earth is like a trading center. Everyone bargains, and that depends on the yardsticks even as quality is the last results. Experience will guide a man, and immaturity will show his follies.

"We watch these interactions from Connuka, you see. Mother Supreme shows mercy to those who work hard, and disposes the lazy ones. Inventions by man are her delights. Challenge her mysteries, and that sickens her. Cardify," Sister Sudan said, "give me the Falcon. If you don't, I will take it and rub you of your position as the chosen one."

Cardify got up, reluctantly, and handed Sister Sudan the Falcon.

She took it and chanted. Two lamps appeared. Then, Sister Sudan uttered a command, and the head of the Falcon opened. A red tube slowly came out of it, and a blue one ascended from the lamp. The tubes interchanged, the blue entered the Falcon while the red, entered the lamp. She repeated the chant ten minutes later, and a red light appeared on the Falcon. After this ritual, Sister Sudan commanded a cloud of smoke that travelled straight into Cardify's mouth.

"You, Cardify, have been empowered with a special charm," Sister Sudan voiced, and disappeared.

Sleep came quickly. Cardify's body went limp and he fell into slumber.

Cardify told no one, until the fullness of time.

CHAPTER FOUR

Cool breeze blew at dawn, swirling sand grains into the open air around Gougee. Forty other villages surrounded Gougee, but it stood the largest village at the base of the Sahara and served as the link between the rainforest and the desert. Frogs were no longer croaking, as the night had been put in the past. Now, chickens and other animals, large and small, were going about scouting for food. Gougee, this community of more than a hundred huts, was slow in waking up from last night's celebrations. The people had celebrated Faoula's marriage, Chief Menka's daughter, to a trader from across the desert. Being an important affair, the food had been prepared in abundance; fifty cows, twenty goats, forty chickens, besides grains, vegetable roots and wine. Neighboring villages bore gifts and dancers performed while this celebration lasted three days.

Commence of the attack on the sleepy village happened swiftly.

Chief Menka's thousand-man army lead by his three commanders, Koinyah, his chief military advisor, Huntoe, the spiritual advisor and Tambo, his private mystical consultant. During the invasion, they had hardly spared a few lives.

Perhaps it was his intuition, but Chief Menka had sent his son, Kpa Por, to Egypt a day before his sister's wedding. It was important that Kpa Por acquire knowledge to continue his father's reign. And, Egypt had the best institutions, so Chief Menka had given his son more than enough gold pieces to cover travel and living expense to last the two years. However, Kpa Por's personal attendant, Borbor Zumbo, had remained to attend the wedding and was to follow later.

Cleanup teams in the north and southeast of Gougee were ordered to report bodies of the dead. There was much to be counted, as Tambo had been made aware on his way to meet Huntoe and Koinyah. Their chief must not wait for long to give his victory speech at the town square.

"Chief Kamauna is ready to address the people," Tambo said to Huntoe. "Where is Koinyah?"

"Taking the final body count," Huntoe replied. "He's only a few meters away."

"You must send a warrior to hurry him up," Tambo insisted.

"Why would Chief Kamauna address the people?" Huntoe asked. "The captives? This is a military operation, not a democracy."

"People are the bedrock of any government," Tambo replied. "Their happiness is found in a leader's progress. Their sorrow? In a leader's condemnation. Which do you subscribe to, Huntoe?"

"You see, Tambo, while planning this military conquest, we did not settle for establishing diplomatic relations with Zenkepa, or Abyssinia, the two greatest spiritual rulers of humankind. You've always known that I will never sit and watch Abyssinia gain favor. Here or any place else. Zenkepa will furbish," Huntoe snapped angrily. "That's it!"

"I see why the sweeping waves of Zenkepa left all those bodies along the road and the town square," Tambo said. "Zenkepa... a spiritual legacy to kill for Cunnuka blessings! Burn others for self realization... love life because of pleasure," he teased.

"We will use this operation to correct those on the wrong path," Huntoe assured. "Those corrupted by spiritual and cultural imaginations are against this revolution. We will cut them off."

"Kill humanity to save humanity? Egocentric apex is the point at which one man judge another man."

"You don't mean well for this revolution, Tambo. Do you? The best generals are those whom the people feared."

"And, out of their fear your nightmare begins," Tambo retorted.

Koinyah arrived at that moment, holding his sword, fresh blood dripping.

Tambo turned to face Koinyah. "Your blade signifies royalty and might," he joked.

"Might is in the blade," Koinyah replied. "It gives power to rule... judge... and punish."

"Power comes from the people," Tambo corrected. "If one kills most of them to gain power, how many will remain to serve the king?"

"A tangible bloc seems to be dividing Zenkepa and Abyssinia," Koinyah replied. "And, Zenkepa is the way forward. I would never jump over that bloc to satisfy the demands of weaklings."

"The mind of the weakling is more powerful than the might of the strong," Tambo quoted. Both men looked at him, but said nothing. "Gentlemen," he said and sighed, "Chief Kamauna is awaiting us in the town square. Shall we go?"

The three men mounted their horses and galloped away, Tambo leading.

Chief Kamauna took his place on a three-foot high mount to address the people.

"My fellow men and people," he began, "King David continued to say, 'Lord, when I consider the heavens, the work of your fingers, the moon and the stars, which you have ordained; what is man, that you are mindful of him? And the son of man, that you visit him? For you have made him a little lower than the angels, and has crowned him with glory and honor. You made him to have dominion over the works of your hands; you put all things under his feet; O Lord, how excellent is your name in all the earth.'

"The Koran says, 'Praise belongs to God, the Lord of all beings, the All merciful, the All-compassionate, the master of the Day of Doom. O Thee, only we serve.'

"And the Master said, 'He who rules by moral force is like the pole-star, which remains in its place while all the lesser stars do homage to it.'

"The words of Confucius, my fellow men, those are words of wisdom. Every man is entitled to subscribe to any, but I will always join King David and say, 'I will sing of loyalty and of justice; to thee, O Lord, I will sing.'"

The people listened.

"Abyssinia has been our forefather, our friend, since the planning of this conquest," Chief Kamauna continued. "This great nation with such strong spiritual ideology, has provided us with guidance within every facet of our existence. I believe in Abyssinia and its rules of laws. Moreover, I believe in an individual's freedom... his will to develop his mind... his speech... and to enhance the comfort of his dwelling place. I will make sure to provide these conditions for the people of Gougee!

"This revolution took away the lives of loved ones and enemies alike," Chief Kamauna continued. "Beware, war means death, and those departed will forever be remembered."

The people remained quiet, but obviously pleased.

"In remembrance of those departed, I declared all loots taken by my men be given back to their rightful owners," Chief Kamauna went on. "We will divide the town into three regions, each controlled by one of my three commanders. A twelve-man council, consist of men of this town, will work with the commander of each region. The council will decide cases, and decide how they want to be governed. I am the commander in chief, and will meet with my commanders, and heads from each council, quarterly. The fate of Gougee will be discussed.

"Magicians and herbalists must group themselves to serve the people and the kingdom. Skilled men must unite and think of ways to do unimaginable things. And now to my men, I say thanks, but we still have a lot more to do to expand this noble town. People of Gougee, all of you, go and live in peace. Your sorrow is my sorrow... and, your joy, my joy. I thank you," Chief Kamauna finished.

Some men raised their swords, and those who didn't, shouted joyously. Their roars echoed far and beyond.

"Did you hear that?" Huntoe asked Koinyah, as they headed toward their horses.

"Our chief is a weakling these days," Koinyah snapped. "It seems he has made a speech to satisfy the conquest, and at the same time, aggravate the conquerors."

"And make the revolution meaningless," Huntoe added. "Where have you heard, or seen, the conquerors return the spoils? Their benefits? When we conquer, we keep the spoils. It's ours. What has gotten into Chief Kamauna's head?"

Koinyah looked at him. "Tambo, of course," he said. "It's his stupid doctrine of people-first. Lately, Chief Kamauna has been listening to him. I've heard that Tambo and Chief Kamauna have been in private talks with an envoy from Abyssinia."

Huntoe's eyes widened.

"If the chief will continue with such attitude," Koinyah continued, "happiness and pleasure will weep. Integrity is forever doomed. We need an alternative." He held Huntoe's eyes without a blink.

The man offered no word or reaction.

"I see you do not cherish the rule of laws," Koinyah went on. "I dislike it too."

Koinyah thought for a moment. "Huntoe, what did the chief tell the delegation from Zenkepa?" he asked, after collecting his thoughts.

"You mean the meeting held several years ago?"

Koinyah nodded.

"I'm surprised that this occurred to you," Huntoe said. "The chief said there are two ideologies ruling the world. Abyssinia, so-called, rules of laws and Zenkepa, Pseudo-Communism. However, Abyssinia has won."

"Abyssinia has won?" Koinyah barked. "Why wasn't I told?"

"Perhaps we've been overlooked, you and I," Huntoe suggested. "By Chief Kamauna and Tambo."

Koinyah furrowed his brow.

"Now they run the show," Huntoe continued. "I paved the way

SHEDRICK B. SETON

for this revolution… I betrayed my own people when I travelled to the south to inform you all about the enormous resources in this town. And, it was you, Koinyah, whose influence made it possible to recruit the right men for the task. Where were Chief Kamauna and Tambo?"

"Chanting in the temple of brotherhood," Koinyah mocked.

"It doesn't matter if the priests plan and we implement," Huntoe said angrily. "The fact is, warriors can also be good planners. No man must take away our rights… not even our chief."

It took only a moment for Koinyah to process Huntoe's reasoning.

"Huntoe," Koinyah said, "I want you to re-establish contact with the emissary from Zenkepa… at any cost. Tell them that Gougee's senior commander, Kionyah, would like to establish diplomatic ties with their country. However, Zenkepa must support our plan to take Gougee from the claws of Chief Kamauna and his spiritual leader, Tambo… and those of Abyssinia."

"Koinyah," Huntoe said, and smiled. "I have already had a discussion with the emissary. They seemed to be in support of such a plan. And, you, Koinyah, are the greatest general in our time."

* * * *

One week later, Huntoe got permission from Chief Kamauna so he would travel back to the south to recruit more men for future conquests. The road trip lasted three weeks before reaching Zenkepa. Like a globe on its axis, the hanging kingdom sat on what looked like a broom straw midway in the misty rainforest. Its only

46

entrance was at the base of a tree trunk. This spiritual town was the greatest, south of the Sahara. Zenkepa, though a modest town, presided over the largest empire consisting of one hundred twenty-two kingdoms and states. The people sort Zenkepa for spiritual guidance, instead of Abyssinia. Mother Supreme favored the land, and when Sister Sudan came to earth, she had settled on the spot on which the worship center stood. It was also believed that Sister Sudan brought Futu Jallon along, the wizard she created while in Connuka. Futu Jallon had spanned several concoctions into motion which randomly selected a few persons with extra wisdom to build the worship center. They built other infrastructures too.

Sister Sudan created several kings and made them leaders over these kingdoms. Every king went to her for spiritual guardian, and reassurances. She assumed Africa to be a lone continent; where trees waved freely, animals and man were created equal. But man was free to kill, as he wished.

Everything was in place as Mother Supreme had planned it, and anyone questioning its operations, or growth or development, was charged with heresy. Governance was Sister Sudan's responsibility, as was her descendents. Though all wealth belonged to Mother Supreme, who had sent The Falcon to earth, it was Sister Sudan who managed it, being it's spiritual guide. Everyone, man or animal, kings and kingdoms, in need of spiritual transformation and stability, are to continue paying tithes to Sister Sudan or her descendents.

This, of course, was against Mother Supreme's will. No one was to worship another deity, or question Sister Sudan, or her descendents, on how the spiritual, political, and material natures of the continent were to be handled. Violators were excommunicated; no trading partners or recognition from other kingdoms. Destruction of peace and security would follow, and their benefits from Cunnuka would be denied. But since Sister Sudan disappeared from earth, Zenkepa had been governed by several spiritual heads with Zoe titles. She had not left an heir, so Futu Jallon gathered twenty-four wise men at the castle. They had come from around the kingdoms and states so that a successor would be chosen.

Bon du, the first Zoe, came from the kingdom of Kandefa. The twenty-three others were called Pa-Zoe, representing all kingdoms, and replaced only by death. They assisted the Chief Zoe, who had absolute power. Since Zoes had the power to decide for mankind, the Chief Zoe decreed that Zoes were spiritual and infallible. Everyone, including Pa-zoes and kings, were to wear the almighty tattoo. Every man was to bow to the Chief Zoe when he passes by. They were to ask him for forgiveness, rather than go to Cunnuka. He held the power to forgive man's sins, and upon man's death, he was certain of going into a city state called, Post Existence. Sister Sudan had created the city to separate the good from the bad. Two roads connected the city to Cunnuka and the city of the abyss.

Those who read the decree knew that it was completely different from the original dorsea from Cunnuka. Man would have to appeal for forgiveness on earth, and in the City of Post Existence, thus making the road to joy and condemnation a far fetch reality. But none dare to speak about it and risk being thrown into the burning forest.

After several years, the quest for the position of Chief Zoe, or Pa- Zoes, was determined by the strongest and richest kingdoms. The desire for wealth and political authority, even vengeance, scraped the position out of its essence. The wealthiest with several kingdoms penetrated the rank and file of the system, and influence decisions. Greedy politicians in powerful kingdoms, with the authority of the Chief Zoe, stumbled upon weak city states. During the age of Huntoe, Zenkepa was governed by Zoe Zeobon Kaiflay.

Huntoe entered Zenkepa and was met by the chief spiritual, Zoe Zeobon Kaiflay and the residents. Cone-shaped houses in town were lined in this formation; seven in front, seven behind, and twelve in the back. Giant trees hung over the town, shielding it from the sun. Home to about two hundred persons, Zenkepa's history dates back to the beginning of creation. The human race had evolved out of the guidance of Mr. Spider, known as BpaSam. After creating several species, Mother Supreme decided to take a break in the middle of the week, so she went for a walk. Later, she sat under a tree and began molding clay in her hand, adding saliva from her mouth. This process went on until BpaSam, the Tarantula, was formed.

"With these eight eyes and eight legs, I command you to guide mankind," said Mother Supreme. "Your name will forever remain in the folklore of this continent."

It was here, where Sister Sudan landed. And, it was here, where Zenkepa came to life.

✳ ✳ ✳ ✳

Chief Zoe Zeobon and Huntoe walked through Zenkepa until they entered the Fortune Tree. They sat around the great fire of Gbeee.

"What brings you here," Zeobon asked Huntoe.

"I would like to make an arrangement," Huntoe replied.

Chief Zoe Zeobon nodded, encouraging Huntoe to go on.

"It would be good for Guogee to be under the guidance and protection of Zenkepa," Huntoe suggested in low whispers.

Chief Zoe brought his ear closer.

"We will need you there," Huntoe continued. "When we take over, everyone will have to take the Almighty Tattoo and submit to the will of Zenkepa."

Chief Zoe Zeobon let out a chuckle. "I have something to show you," he said, and pulled out some document.

Huntoe took it.

"Guogee is very strategic to us," Chief Zoe Zeobon informed. "You would have to go through the Great Door to get to spiritual awareness and meet with the spirits for blessing. After your meeting, you can squeeze this bead to take you back to Gougee," he handed Huntoe a red bead.

After his meeting with Chief Zoe Zeobon, Huntoe walked to the Great Door made of palm straws, and gave the red bean a squeeze.

* * * *

"Everything is set," Huntoe said to Koinyah. "Zenkepa is willing to train our men for this covert activity, and if we wish, it will also send soldiers to assist us in taking over the affairs of state. Zenkepa wants to maintain its presence in this region and we must be willing to aid the country in reaching its goals of keeping Abysannia out of here. We are to allow the royal team from Zenkepa to travel freely throughout our region. Traders from Zenkepa will help in strengthening our economy. They will open the biggest salt export business, followed by specialists to train us in using the newest ideology, 'unity through communal activities' to support its One for all, All for one policy.

"Zenkepa also wants to build the biggest spider web."

"Spider web?"

"To monitor and protect us from flies and other poisonous insects from Abyssinian. We need to provide strategic land," Huntoe ended his report.

"Tell your trusted men to meet me next week in my region," Kionyah ordered.

"Yes, Sir."

"Wait a minute," Kionyah said, as Huntoe walked away.

Huntoe stopped.

"Thank you, Huntoe," Kionyah said. "You have done well."

It pleased Huntoe. His chest puffed out with pride.

* * * *

Due to Gougee's strategic position, and several natural resources, Zenkepa and Abysianna secretly dispatched emissaries to establish relationship. These great spiritual powers, stumbling for international supremacy, needed the likes of Gougee to boast universal dominance. Abyssinia was preaching (on behalf of Mother Supreme) that individual freedom will expand trade and commerce, and one freed world as a cradle of several choices. On the other hand, Zenkepa preached (on behalf of Sister Sudan) how a controlled communal engagements will lead to a world filled with equal opportunities. It has been ages since these powers, Zenkepa in the west and Abyssinia in the east, had been preaching these counter engagements. But as the world advanced,

Zenkepa strategy switched, making only a few to move up the food chains and assured maximum protection. This triggered a mass exodus of individuals and nations to crossover, placing Zenkepa's power above Abyssinia. A few people, and nations, still admired Abyssinia's religious doctrine. Tambo was one of those, and he made sure to read all about Abyssinia in the temple.

Chief Kamauna always visited the temple to edify himself. During one of those visits, he met Tambo and grew fond of him. At that time, the two were approached by Kionyah and Huntoe with the plan of conquest. After the capture of Gougee, the two powers sent goodwill notes and emissaries, but Tambo convinced Chief Ka Mauna to refuse Zenkepa and only accept Abyssinia. The Chief asked Zenkepa's emissary to leave Gougee, giving him only twenty-four hours. On their way, they met Huntoe, who showed sympathy, and after having a lengthy discussion, they moved on.

Less than three months after the victory speech, Tambo received an invitation to visit Abyssinia to sign various communiqués.

CHAPTER FIVE

Koinyah and Huntoe had several meetings with military leaders from Zenkepa. A de facto memorandum of understanding, focusing on trade and commerce, security, and education, was signed between Koinyah and Zenkepa. It was also agreed that upon the takeover, Zenkepa would send military advisors to build a new army, set up the economic system and build infrastructure. Koinyah was to pay back all expenses incurred in gold and other valuable minerals. The overthrow of the regime would be coordinated by the Zenkepains and by the break of dawn, the local forces will take over the affairs of security. Zenkepa would have a permanent liaison. It was also agreed that Huntoe would serve as Secretary Extraordinary assigned to Zenkepa. Huntoe went over the plan with the Zenkepains. He was satisfied with it terms and conditions including over throwing Chief Menka and destroying Tambo.

"Koinyah, my lord, the plan is set," Huntoe informed. "Men have been posted off Gougee territory in the western frontier. The Zenkepain generals have brought in more horses, swords and helmets… recruitment and training of men for this operation are completed."

"Good. Good."

"Zenkepa also sent one hundred brawny men along with twenty generals," Huntoe continued. "They advised that we remain on the inside, while they fight from outside."

"Great idea, Huntoe," Koinyah declared.

"What shall we do about the advisors from Abyssinia?"

"They will leave," Koinyah advised. "Abyssinia cannot allow her citizens to die in a sub-Saharan city state. Give the signal to begin the revolution. I am going to the town-square to alert Chief Menka about the attack. This is the only way we can separate him from Tambo. Once the Chief is dead, Tambo will be taken care during the mourning ceremony."

Huntoe furrowed his brow.

"Don't worry, Huntoe," Koinyah said. "I'm going to convince him so that I take a few men east, where you will have an ambush waiting. Once you give the signal, go home quickly just to avoid any suspicion. This day will determine our fate."

＊＊＊＊

"Where is Chief Menka?" Koinyah shouted as he entered the parlor of the compound.

The guard stepped aside.

"Chief, we are under attack," Koinyah announced. "News from the northern frontier confirmed that strange men have attacked our position. I hope they are not Berber Traders."

"Where's Huntoe?" Chief Menka asked. "And, Tambo?"

"Still at home, Chief. I don't think they are aware of the attack." Then, Koinyah turned to the guards. "Go and get the two generals."

Within a short while, Huntoe and Tambo entered the parlor.

"Koinyah informs me that unknown forces have attacked our position in the north," Chief Menka said to Huntoe and Tambo as they marched in.

"How is that possible?" Tambo asked. "There's no city beyond that point. If any one attack from that location, the mountain of sand should wear him down. Besides, Koinyah commands the largest portion of our men in the north... no one could attack where there's high casualty."

"Nonsense," Koinyah barked. "Are you implying me and my men are doing a poor job? Do you know how many men I have lost since last night's attack?"

Tambo said nothing.

"I am losing men left and right," Koinyah continued. "They have a heavy force because they're using modern weapons... applying new methods of fighting."

"No need to argue, Tambo," Huntoe intervened, before Tambo would speak. "Rather than argue, we should be thinking about marshalling men to push back the invaders."

"Perhaps Chief Menka can take a few warriors and attack from the east position," Koinyah suggested. "Tambo and his men will attack from the west, while Huntoe and I will attack from the north."

"You and Huntoe combined forces?" Tambo asked. "Why?"

"We have the largest troops," Huntoe jumped in. "Besides, it would be saving you and Chief Menka, Tambo. We are taking on the most dangerous terrains."

"Then go ahead and plan it," Chief Menka urged. "We're running out of time."

✳✳✳✳

Chief Menka and his men travelled on horseback by way of Donza, a little town about twenty kilometers from Gougee. The town center had been turned into a hiding place, unknown to them, as Chief Menka and his men were attacked as soon as they reached it. The chief and his men handled the surprise attack fearlessly, but losing all his men except about seven. Chief Menka and his remaining seven warriors managed to escape to the desert until they reached an oasis. Except, as they drink from a spring, more than a dozen masked men on donkeys surrounded them. Exhausted from the first attack, and unable to fight back, Chief Menka and his men fell bravely.

✳✳✳✳

At sundown, Huntoe and his men galloped to the town square with Chief Menka's body. The people, including Tambo, inquired of him what had taken place. He informed them that his men had found Chief Menka en route to Donza.

Tambo wept bitterly.

Later that evening, thousands of men assembled at town center for their chief's eulogy. Huntoe, Koinyah and Tambo were in attendance.

"Men of Gougee," Koinyah went first, "I have never admired anyone as much as I have admired our fallen chief. He was a great man… a visionary who loved his people. He was their protector."

The people murmured in agreement.

"He wanted to transform your life," Koinyah continued. "I meant, our lives. Only the Almighty knows a man's thoughts."

Koinyah collected his thoughts, staring at the audience.

They waited patiently to hear more.

"Death," he said and sighed. "That old monster, Death, has taken away all potentials, and many good people, including Chief Menka, at will. Who can question him? Can he be stopped? My tears will forever fall for this great chief… and at such; we ought to erect a statue to commemorate Chief Menka… our brother and father."

The audience erupted with cheers.

"And, whoever committed this murder," Koinyah shouted, "will be brought to justice!"

The people, mostly warriors, began moving their hands with up and down motions, even stomping the ground with clubs. Some began doing their war dance.

Koinyah raised his hand and shouted, "May Chief Menka's soul… and souls of the others, rest in perfect peace!"

The men stood still.

"Long live Menka's soul!" Koinyah shouted.

They cheered until Huntoe walked to the front.

Huntoe took the stand. "Good men of Gougee," he began, "worriers! There's always darkness before dawn. Gougee has suffered enough! Chief Menka's trusted commander, Koinyah, with his men, sought a reason to liberate us. We are freed... free at last! Chief Menka knew that death is unexpected, so he's been preparing a son... a man of honor, to fulfill his dream."

Every eye stared at Huntoe. He had their attention.

"Why shall we mourn?" Huntoe continued. "Chief Menka is seated with the elders, his work on earth is over. Our time has come, so we must govern well. We are saddened by his unexpected death, but at the same time, we must be happy for the man he has left us... a son... a warrior... a future king... Koinyah. Let us rejoice rather than mourn!"

The men cheered as Huntoe stepped aside.

Tambo came forward.

"Two great men have spoken before me," Tambo started. "They have each given praise of a deserving chief. Though giving praise to the dead is an old custom, but is praise for the dead or for the living?"

Tambo had asked merely for effect with no answer expected.

"When a man dies," he continued. "Our ancestors meet him at the entrance of the great door, and shower him with gifts. Each person will receive gifts based on morality and good work. And the living? The living meets the living daily, and will be praised, or criticized, by his deeds... by your deeds, you will win admirers or enemies. You are admired when you're a fool... a down trodden... humble, but with a strong personality, you can succeed. Your life should not be used to threaten other people's surroundings. Do that, and you've won yourself some enemies... that is when you see beyond reasoning and enter other people's surroundings."

Tambo took in his breath and let it out slowly.

"Chief Menka was not a fool, but a far-sighted person," he

continued. "He regarded wealth as something used properly, and not something to boast about. He saw reasons to continue his conquest without interfering in the interest of his victims... his assimilation policy.

"A leader's spoken word must be clear, and concise. If not, the public will misunderstand him. His enemies will use the ignorance of the public to get at him or crush him.

"Good men of Gougee, we should investigate the murder of Chief Menka on our own soil instead of erecting a symbol of praise," Tambo suggested. "The person in charge of this town, is charged with the task to continue the work of Chief Menka."

Huntoe shouted, "Koinyah is the person!"

"Not to my knowledge," Tambo replied. "However, I suggest we set up a council of ten elders. We can choose from the length and breadth of this country to select Chief Menka's successor."

Huntoe and Koinyah exchanged glances.

"Let me ask this," Tambo continued. "Why must the aggression cease upon Chief Menka's death? Why are there more warriors at this occasion than the town's people? Why aren't the warriors in the battlefield?"

"Your questions are out of place," bark Koinyah. "Are you accusing us of wrongdoing?"

"Beware, Tambo... you will be charged with treason," Huntoe declared. "You are inciting the people against the government."

"Get a hold of him!" Koinyah ordered.

A group of combatants rushed to Tambo, but Tambo vanished quicker than a flash of lightning.

Koinyah took charge that day, and as commander in chief, he began extending to the east, across the Sahara, and west toward the jungle. With the passing of time, Gougee was placed under

Zenkepa, and Koinyah became its political leader. Eventually, he changed the name Gougee to Fricano and crowned himself king.

＊＊＊＊

At the appointed time Cardify presented the Falcon to Koinyah, but became its caretaker. Cardify advised the King of The Golden Falcon mystical power. It had been sent to the king to give him extra occult power to lead his people. The Falcon would gather resources from all parts of the continent to make the kingdom rich and powerful. However, every citizen must be allowed to enjoy this gift, as it had come from Mother Supreme through Sister Sudan, whose presence is felt all over Zenkepa.

"Greed... discrimination... even converting your neighbor wife, would lead the kingdom in the wrong direction," Cardify warned.

"What is greed?" Koinyah asked. "And, what is discrimination?"

"Wrongful acquisition of everything," replied Cardify. "But you are the king and you control everything. Whatever you do cannot be considered as greed, and to whom you give, does not mean you are discriminating. In this kingdom, you are everyone's father... and by law, every woman is your bride."

Koinyah ordered a building built, including a massive hall, to host Cradify and the Falcon. An adjacent hall would be used for the Convert Ceremony. Supreme occult power was given Koinyah by the combined powers of the magicians in the region, that he could be seen in many places at the same time. Huntoe added that the first harvest of all would be brought to the king for his blessing.

All first born, except the king's and his senior officials, would be sacrificed to the gods of the harvest, sunshine, and long life.

It wasn't too long until the town became a killing field. A law was passed that everyone addressed the king with the title, Loutia, meaning half god, half man. Koinyah was greeted as, 'Loutia Koinyah' or 'O King'. The title had supernatural power, when mentioned, the individual's personality would leave him and enter the king, making him so powerful that people fell when he shouted at them. He molested his subjects' wives and made an open show of them. Fricano had gold and salt, becoming the biggest donors to Zenkepa. The manner in which King Koinyah was governing his subjects, was his prerogative. And, Zenkepa turned its face.

The king's regular tour around the kingdom was filled of pageantry. He travelled with five hundred golden chariots always, and the one thousand horses Zenkepa donated. The horses were decorated with attractive materials, and the riders looked magnificent. Two thousand armed soldiers protected the king; with spears, bows and shields. King Koinyah's personal attendants, mostly women, wore red gowns with golden strips around the sleeves and hems. There were twenty chosen beautiful girls, half-naked, whose job was to sprinkle gold dust in front of the king's chariot as it moved. Musicians sang in harmony with the dancers. This spectacle was witnessed by the entire kingdom, as the inhabitants of each town lined the main roads just to catch a glimpse of the king and his attendants.

King Koinyah organized his government into three branches: the Royal, the Judiciary and the People. The Royal Branch consisted of the king and his advisors, including immediate family members, princes and sons of princes whose residence was a triangular-shape building around the royal square. A hall connected the royal palace to the advisors building, which served as a secret passage to meet directly with the king. These advisors were considered noble and holy, as every citizen bowed to them whenever they passed them in the town square and market places.

A component of the advisors was military men who fought alongside Koinyah during the conquest of the north. They were now commanding officers, and laws were enacted by the judiciary. The advisors headed the other branches of government and controlled the four regions of the kingdom. As for Huntoe, King Koinyah made him his assistant for state affairs. Huntoe had oversight of finance, security, education, justice, social, and all segments of the kingdom. And, magicians oversaw the king's personal attendants.

Huntoe compiled the Judiciary with soldiers, and put them over the courts in every city. Militiamen in reserve were also part of the judiciary. The Judiciary handled criminal and civil cases and decided punishment. An-eye-for-an-eye resulted in most cases.

He advised King Koinyah to have the People's Branch deal with construction and farming only; manufacturing farm tools and weapons of war, but this was kept under several surveillance. They had an annual review of the branch activities.

Hunter persuaded citizens into believing that King Koinyah was infallible and fearing, so when young boys under eleven years of age were enlisted into the army for special military training called Rebass, not one parent objected. Rebass training comprised of the tactics in warfare, handling of war weapons and special military drills. However, children of officials, and children gifted with talents in warfare, were sent to Zenkepa for special training.

Koinyah had the message, Dead men cannot see the passing of time; life is a gainful venture, carved on wooden plates and hung it all public venues and citizen's home. A Palava hut was built with an underground vault, which kept Chief Menka's body. One room was used for offering gifts in fruits and fine materials to the chief's spirit, believed to appear once a year inquiring of Gougee's welfare. This Palava hut also served as the place to settle disputes between the king and senior officials of the revolution.

$$* * * *$$

Before long, Kpa Por had been informed by a trader regarding the attack on Gougee. He was aware his home was now called, Fricano. His parents, with many other villagers, had been massacred. However, he'd been informed that his wife and his foster father were alive. Fearing for his life, Kpa Por left Egypt and crossed the Mediterranean Sea into the Greek Province. He hired a private tutor on the outskirt of Sparta to teach him different military tactics. And, during his study at the academy, he befriended Abuka, the son of a wealthy Berber trader. After his training, Kpa Por and Abuka occasionally sneaked into the marketplace to listen to different discourses. One day in the marketplace, he heard Socrates argued with some elites from Pericles court, which was surprising. How could someone of such lowly origin outwit people in high places with his discourses?

Kpa Por's spear-throwing and combat skills had no match in Sparta. Head of his class, his trainers took a special likeness to him. However, Kpa Por was mostly influenced by free-spirited Abuka. He and Abuka often disguised as traders and travelled to Athens for pleasure. It was during one of these trips when they met Socrates in a discourse with the elites. Socrates turned toward a group of young men, including Kpa Por and Abuka, and asked, "What is life?"

"The ability to live," a bystander replied.

Socrates laughed.

"I believe it is the act of living," Kpa Por offered.

Socrates turned his eye on him. "I am ignorant to what constitute living," he said, "but does living constitute having military might? Or encouraging a free spirit? Living?"

Kpa Por held his peace.

"We all live in Athens City State, where slaves and the elite live," Socrates said. "Does the difference show how the republic is stratified? Aren't we constantly told, from birth until death, that we are Athenians? Athens is a free city state and a democracy… a land of the freed. Isn't it a place where great men congregate to unleash their skills… their abilities and professionalism?

"The painter is free… the writer is free… the dramatic is free. Everyone is freed. Free?"

No one said a word. Socrates smiled.

"What is freedom if all the great works of arts are patronized by Pericles and the elites," he asked. "The oracle of Delphi… does it not tell you what is suitable to your ears? How worthy are you? How can you aspire to be what you want to be? When slaves, citizens and elites consult the oracle, what are their readings? The Oracle will tell you, Socrates loves the good life, but he will live this good life within his limited life-zone. A slave is a slave, and he can live the good life in his limited life-zone. So, can you compare the lifestyles of Pericles and the elites to those of the citizens or slaves?"

"Many Athenians," Socrates knocked his right hand into his left palm, gesticulating. "Cannot still live with the facts that in this democracy slaves and masters are dining at the same table. It is not unlawful, but they preserved it as unlawful and brainwash this generation that a man slave who laid with a female Athenian is an abomination to Apollo and his heavenly hosts. He must be stoned to death; but Apollo accepts as lawful a mating between the master and the female slaves. Athen is aware that this is its greatest evil and weakness, but refused to accept the principle that all men are created equal. Arthan also boosts of its democracy as the cradle for a peaceful world, but allow pride to blind its judgement and its Achilles heel, fear to completely accept and assimilate slaves into it social structure, will destroy all its pillars. If Athen is not careful, two forces-internal (failure to completely incorporate slaves and external-foreign policy of mentally bullying other nations) will lead to its destruction.

This deliberation got their attention. As Socrates went on, Kpa Por's mind drifted to Fricano and its system of governance, as well as their lifestyles. His encountered with Socrates was an eye opener, a renewal of spirit, and an enlightenment; a rebirth. Kpa Por visited Athens regularly, thereafter, attending Socrates' deliberations wherever the great master preached. One year later, he completed his training and returned to Fricano.

* * * *

Huntoe, now the Epicenter of the kingdom, had his tentacles in every agency and department, as well as household. He had ears everywhere. People were paid to spy on each other, even family members. The culprits were now punished by Gbodu, a special intelligence squad. Every citizen, before going to Zenkepa for his identity mark, sought approval from Huntoe's office. He decided how much one earned, and how much tax one had to pay.

Fricano was now a rich and powerful city state across the Mediterranean Sea when Kpa Por returned. The government established an import and export tax system for all goods bought and taken out of the kingdom. A monetary system, copied from Zenkepa, enabled traders from other city states to trade in the kingdom. Investors came in by the hundreds to honor the king's free of charge investment—come, get, and give mine policy. Many explored and exploited the gold, diamond, crude oil, the vast forest and several other natural minerals. However, no investor was told to build a processing plant because the king considered his kingdom a free and needing exposure. It became a mandate that any investor entering Fricano get a supervising advisor from the advisor square to work with. The decree was that the supervising advisor would get sixty percent of the profit, dividing this among himself, the government and the king.

This arrangement, once approved by the investor, would make his investment exempt from lawsuits and be protected from other investment unfriendly situation. As a result, most investors started exploiting the kingdom's resources to cover up their expenses. They bribed local supervisors and exported more quantity of the resources. Advisors and local supervisors started building beautiful houses in the city, and bribed Huntoe's office to approve the renting of their buildings to the government and incoming investors. Other investors brought in beautiful clothes, jewelries and arts from the Orient to those in high places. This move provided them sole considerations during the tax payment season and the justice system. Money entering the kingdom's treasury was controlled and used by Huntoe. Advisors, controlling other towns, were benefiting from gifts from investors; wearing beautiful and expensive clothes and beads from city states in Asia Minor.

To promote and maintain massive food production, while controlling and monitoring those within the People Branch, the government ordered forced communal farming in all towns except Fricano and Koita, the second city. During harvest, all crops were sent to the House of Food in Fricano which had a subsidiary unit all over the kingdom. The House of Food was structured to store large quantity of food, with power to regulate on a daily basis the quantity each household to eat.

Huntoe ordered all children and parents at the bottom of the food chain, and living in Fricano, to work in the making of spears, gallops, and other weapons of war. In as much as the restriction was stringent, young people from the surrounding towns camouflaged themselves or bribed their way to Koita, the second biggest city, in search of greener pasture. Most became conscripts of the army of unemployed.

Due to the influx, labor became cheap and prices of goods and services increased, thus affecting the cost of living. This led to higher crime rate, and every night, there was news of burglary or an attempt in every neighborhood. Investors soon demanded more military presence as the constant theft and strikes by employees began to hamper their operations.

Kpa Por took a job at the dory and the shield manufacturing shop, and soon Huntoe was informed that he was the son of the late chief of Gougee. Huntoe immediately put Kpa Por under extreme surveillance. Kpa Por felt discouraged, but his only inspiration was in Youjay, his wife, and his foster father who often narrated the story of Gougee and then, Fricano.

Kpa Por's mother had met Youjay at the public oasis, and

after several interactions, decided to meet with the girl's parents. She marked Youjay as a possible bride for her son, and before his departure to Egypt, Kpa Por and Youjay were married. Youjay's natural beauty drew everyone's attention; an oval shaped face with sleepy eyes and radiant lips. Her smiles were a gentle nature that displayed dimples in both cheeks, the point of her attraction. Kpa Por was fond of her and they spent most evenings together; walking, playing and even singing among the Savanna grass.

Every day at twilight, Youjay met Kpa Por at the entrance of his workplace and they would walk home together holding hands. Many admired their relationship, and soon they were role models for younger people. Whenever there were confusions in the town, the judge would use Youjay and Kpa Por's relationship as an example of a better relationship.

One weekend Huntoe decided to tour the towns, west and north of Fricano. During this tour, he decided to stop where the weapons were being manufactured. Huntoe saw Youjay awaiting her husband at the entrance, and was immediately moved by her beauty.

"What are you doing here," Huntoe greeted Youjay when he reached her.

She bowed and replied, "I've come to meet my husband, My Lord."

"Women are forbidden where weapons of war are manufactured," Huntoe said. "Do you not know?"

"I was not told, My Lord," Youjay replied. "I usually meet my husband out here and we go home together."

"Who is your husband?"

"Kpa Por, My Lord."

"Well," Huntoe sighed. "He has broken the laws of the shrine…
and must be punished. The penalty is death."

Youjay gasped.

"By hanging," Huntoe added. "And, his wife taken."

Youjay's eyes well with tears.

"Arrest Kpa Por and take him to the dungeon for an early
hanging tomorrow morning," Huntoe ordered. "Take her to the
king castle," he pointed at Youjay. "Put her in the widows' quarters."

Youjay broke down.

Kpa Por struggled to free himself as he was dragged out of
his workplace, and even more, when Youjay was put into Huntoe's
chariot.

Soon, news about Kpa Por and Youjay's arrest spread
throughout Fricano like angry bees. The more the story was told,
or re-told, it took on a new version. One version showed that
Huntoe had seen Kpa Por as the people's savior and he was to bring
hope and stop their suffering. So, Huntoe had decided to kill him.
Another version showed that Kpa Por was captured because of his
wife's beauty. Yet, others believed it was because of the constant
injustice from the administration.

Later that day, people started to move around appealing for
the release of Kpa Por and Youjay. As expected, Huntoe sent
warriors to calm the situation. And, as expected, several persons
were killed, and property damaged or looted. Huntoe took Youjay
to the palace and turned her over to the king. Immediately King
Koinyah saw Youjay, like a magnetic force, her beauty ceased all of
his consciousness.

"She will be my twelfth wife," the king told Huntoe. He nodded.
"This evening is the usual condomnation ceremony. You know
what to do," King Koinyah added.

That evening, as Huntoe had ordered, Kpa Por was brought to the king's bed chamber, naked.

"Well," Huntoe greeted the prisoner. "It is time that you, young lover… or should I say, hero, see the difference between power and love."

To Kpa Por's dismay, the king raped his wife before his eyes, violently. Youjay wept bitterly. And Kpa Por, standing before the king's bed, his hands and feet tied, wept as well.

"I will marry Youjay," King Koinyah said to Kpa Por, when he was finally done. "She will rule with me. It is already a decreed… and has been sent to every part of the kingdom."

Kpa Por was later taken back to his cell.

The next morning, Kpa Por's cell was found empty. However, people throughout the kingdom never believe that Kpa Por had escaped. They believed Kpa Por had been secretly killed and his body, burned.

Young people in Fricano began showing their frustration and anger in arranging demonstrations. Clashes between warriors and protesters drew an order from the king to have people arrested, or slaughtered. Three hundred persons were captured and killed, and this situation aggravated the residents in the north and west. Citizens grouped themselves and attacked investors and industries in their areas. The warriors repelled the attack and occupied the north and west. More people were captured and killed.

Advisors from the north and west held a meeting, and decided to petition the king to prosecute Huntoe and all involved in the killing of citizens. They requested that he withdraw his army from the north and west, and urged the king to build spiritual schools, and that salt be locally manufactured, gold and diamond be processed locally, and the region producing the minerals or resources, receive twenty percent on taxes paid.

Unexpectedly, King Kionyah executed all the advisors who forwarded the petition. Zenkepa commanded the king to release all the advisors, and called a dialogue throughout the kingdom. However, King Kionyah refused.

Sporadic fighting started in protest of the execution of the advisors, magicians and herbalists from the north and west. Civilians in other regions joined the protest; rebels hijacked traders and at times, adopted them. People from the capital could no more trade with people of other towns. This situation made the highest spiritual leader of the north, Korluba, Kpa Por's foster father, burst into the courtroom during the Convest ceremony, and predicted the fall of Fricano. Korluba was arrested and taken to the Forbidden Forest, and his remains were eaten by the king and his higher ups. Korluba's head was placed in the city square to warn law breakers. After that, there were either sporadic, or gorilla fighting in all parts of Fricano. The trade routes across the Sahara, and routes to Zenkepa, were never free of ambushes.

Some years after, a great army of Barber horsemen, commanded by Kpa Por and Abuka, captured and destroyed Fricano. King Kionyah was captured in bed with a teenage girl and killed. Huntoe disappeared. The old man and the Falcon were never found.

CHAPTER SIX

"When are you leaving Mali, Mr. Nagbe?" Snoteh asked.

"I'd like to get some rest first before leaving for Liberia," Nagbe replied. "And, thanks for helping me with those arts, Snoteh. My boss will be happy."

Snoteh smiled. "Always glad to help a brother out," he said. "Now when I go back to Liberia and visit the museum and see these arts on display, it will give me great joy."

"When are you coming back?"

"Maybe within another two or three years."

Surprised, Nagbe asked, "You plan on spending another two years in this country?"

"Liberia is still at the cross road, Mr. Nagbe," Snoteh sighed. "I mean, anything can happen. Besides, I don't want to go back to

Liberia looking like a rag. I'd like to go back with enough money, and a better education."

Nagbe turned to look at Snoteh. "You can never have enough," he said. "No one can ever get enough money, I mean. Are you in school?"

Rather than say anything, Snoteh scratched the back of his head.

"I'm sorry if I've embarrassed you," Nagbe apologized. "You must have already put action to your thought."

Snoteh only listen. His attention was on the noisy gravels hitting the undercarriage of the car.

"Are you okay?" Nagbe asked.

Snoteh stole a peek at his passenger, then quickly turned his attention back to the road. He continued to listen to the noise underneath the car. Strange enough, the sound changed from crushing rocks to the medley of a talking drum. The rhythms of other drums joined it, then came the sound of taps against empty glass bottles. People added their voices to the music.

They are singing in Bassa, Snoteh thought, recognizing the language. It was the Gbema. Then the language changed to highlight chorus in the Kru language. Snoteh smiled. Nagbe had turned his head and observed.

The car shook awkwardly. Quite noticeably in fact; it sank into an ocean of sand. As if they had been plunged into a new page of life, or a new world, Nagbe and Snoteh could see stone houses far ahead. People were dressed in colorful lappas as they moved about. No one spoke. Not even a whisper was heard. Snoteh opened his mouth to speak. Nothing came out. Nagbe, too, sat mute.

The wind pressure increased, vigorously shaking the car. Simultaneously, the current of air whirling violently upward in a spiral motion built the gathering sand into a mountain. A door at its base opened and a man, dressed in a long white gown, came out. His tall, six-foot-six frame matched his broad shoulders. The front of the man's head, from the top of his forehead to the bottom of his chin, was relatively large with a wry look. He had a pointy nose attentive eyes. The man walked to the car and placed his right hand on Snoteh's face, putting him to sleep. Snoteh's head moved forward and rested it on the steering wheel.

He turned his attention to Nagbe. "Hello, Nagbe."

Nagbe, who seemed unconscious, awoke.

"I am Gbugbe," the man said. "I was sent by Mother Supreme. She loves Liberia, you see. She loves Liberia a lot and cried bitterly when the civil war happened. Mother Supreme was also embarrassed… seeing Liberians killing themselves by the dozens."

Nagbe, in a stupor, tried moving his eyelashes.

"Sister Congo, Sister Sudan's grandchild, asked me to give you this," he continued, and handed the Falcon to Nagbe."

Nagbe took hold of the statue and admired its beauty.

"Sister Congo could have sent it to Nigeria after the Biafra war," he continued, "but Nigeria has been ruled continuously by military rulers. It does not prove good for the people."

Nagbe looked up at the man wide-eyed.

"Our concern is Liberia," he continued. "The Negro republic… or the virgin country, although old in age. Liberia will stand as a light to the rest of the continent. The land for the oppressed and brokenhearted. She will grow strong and her name will be greater than those of Nigeria, South Africa, and even Gabon, if, and only if, the president, or you, will do what the Falcon requires. You are to present this Falcon to the president personally upon your return. He must make an animal sacrifice to it every six month," he added sternly.

Nagbe listened.

"Actually, the animal sacrifice required is six white rams after every two months," Gbugbe continued. "Liberia lost too much blood… the Lutheran Church, Carter Camp, Todee and Cowfield massacres. The fall of Gbarnga, the Johnson's war in Monrovia and other places where people were killed indiscriminately, are reasons for the reduction in the sacrifice. After the sacrifice is done, Liberia will be rich and powerful. She will grow in might like Ancient Fricano. Tell the president that the gift from Mother Supreme must be for the well being of the people, and not for a selected few. It must not be used to fuel the destruction of people. If that happens, or the sacrifice is not done at all, woe unto the people and the land. Goodbye, Nagbe."

Gbugbe disappeared in that instant.

Nagbe and Snoteh regained consciousness, sensing they were sitting in the parked car in front the hotel.

"I know I've been driving," Snoteh said, "But I feel as if I just woke up."

"Well, sleepy head," Nagbe replied, "let me get my bag… we're going to the airport."

"Right now?"

"Yes."

Nagbe got his bag, and was soon on a plane headed to Liberia.

✳ ✳ ✳ ✳

Fricano had been divided among several factions, Youjay

had reunited with her husband, and Kpa por had realized he could not reunite the entire kingdom without further bloodshed; thousand had already lost their lives. He divided the landmass into seven administrative segments, and appointed each of his seven commanders ruler over each unit. And as general overseer, he decreed each component to operate independent of the Fricano. It meant they could run their own show—impose taxes, make their own decision concerning trade, commerce and governance. However, in time of war, they would combine forces. All they needed Fricano for, was to constantly engage Zenkepa for spiritual guidance and global affiliation. The main concern was how they would demilitarize combatants who, for four years, had been in the jungles and towns fighting warriors of the kingdom.

* * * *

Siren haled from the direction of the coming presidential motorcade as cars, as well as pedestrians, hurriedly clear the road. Traveling well over speed of more than 50-MPH, Special Detective Agency (SDA) vehicles leading the motorcade moved from lane to lane, each followed by two jeeps with oversized tires, as they drove pass cars. Most were unaware that the jeeps, equipped with weapons-detector computer systems, were capable of screening metallic objects in other vehicles.

Eight Harley-Davidson motorcycles followed the two jeeps; two ahead of a limousine, two on each side and two at the back. Six Defender jeeps carrying heavily armed police task forces followed the limousine. Another six military patrol mini-jeeps sped along. The army personnel in the mini-jeeps wore red colored over-all with black berets. These were the Terrorist Repel Unit, or TRU, trained in different military disciplines, responsible to guard the Executive Mansion.

Security system put in place to protect the president was indeed unyielding. Task force police would line the streets from morning to night if the president was to pass that road. Police officers were trained every month in anti-terrorist tactics to protect the major highways. The highways were dangerous to travel, humans were murdered and properties stolen. Because of this, a patrol unit was established as a department within the police force. Journalists wrote, as they observed that the security system was the best in modern time.

$$* * * *$$

Nagbe had been promoted to the position of General Secretary of the Department of Tourism. He had made several attempts to deliver the Falcon to the president in person, but to no avail. Security personnel at the Mansion refused him entry, even accusing him of trying to endanger the chief executive because he had refused to deliver the Falcon through another person.

"I have something in my possession that I'd like to show the president," Nagbe said to Johnny Lowee, bodyguard to the Security Director for presidential affairs. "But security won't let me. Everyone wants me to give a purse before granting me access."

"Show me," Johnny replied, and followed Nagbe home.

Nagbe took him to the room where he kept the Falcon. Blue rays of light dangled around the statue. The golden portion shine like blue diamond, lighting the entire room.

"Where did you get it?" Johnny Lowee asked.

"Mali, when I traveled to Timbuktu to buy arts for the museum."

"This could make you a lot of money, Nagbe."

"Really?" Nagbe said. "Who would buy this?"

"I know some guys who are friends with some US Marines at the embassy," Johnny Lowee said. "They could find a buyer. My share will roll. Would you accept a deal?"

"I really can't sell this Falcon," Nagbe said, after giving some thought. "It's divine."

"Divine?" Johnny Lowee said incredulously.

Nagbe nodded. "It was purposely sent to Liberia," he assured. "My home," he added. "The motherland… the one I've prayed for good to befall upon. The next generation will remember me if I do a good job."

Suddenly, ray of blue light dangling around the Falcon changed into a chain of stars. The stars circled Nagbe's head like a crown. Then one star grew in size and remained over his head like a king's crown. Johnny Lowee stiffened in the mean time, his head being pushed to look upward by some unknown force. He stared at the Falcon wide-eye, while red lights shot out of the star over Nagbe's head and headed toward Johnny's eyes. Nagbe's head turned white as an angle's garment while the rest of him looked sky blue. The blueness turned dull, and the room suddenly reeked with dead animal's stench. Johnny Lowee's body melted like hot chocolate.

The star disappeared and Nagbe regained consciousness. But the memory of Johnny Lowee had been erased by the Falcon. He stared down at the brown liquid he had stepped in and tracked the floor.

THE FALCON

∗ ∗ ∗ ∗

Kpa Por opened Fricano to all city states beyond the Mediterranean Sea, those who wished to trade with his kingdom. Abuka, his friend, helped set a self-reliance plan that would make the kingdom self-sufficient. He created avenues allowing citizens to reach their full potential, demobilizing and rehabilitating those fought during the crisis. Anyone could own land if he works with the government, tilling the land and planting crops for seven years. Or own cattle if he breeds two generations of cattle from a single parent. Ownership of gold pits, salt, or precious stones, were outsourced to honest, patriotic citizens of Fricano. Trade routes to Egypt, and city states beyond the Mediterranean, increased profits. Even a middle class of citizens grew out of this, trading in goods and services. Some traded slaves.

Abuka's self-reliance plan seemed a partial solution because there remained many unemployed youths; the crime rates increased. Intermittent revolts sprung up in several city states in Fricano and those closer to Zenkepa, which had now extended its spiritual grips to Egypt and across the Mediterranean Sea; Asia Minor and Europa. People in those states needed Zenkepa, which would connect them to Mother Supreme's throne in the heavens. Leaders visited the west frequently, into holy shrine to acquire the almighty tattoos.

A historian in Fricano wrote: As Fricano is experiencing internal growth; Zenkepa is connecting the world spiritually. All leaders of city states are rulers, but the Chief Zoe on his high stool in Zenkepa is the supreme ruler of rulers.

Kingdoms grew and declined in the Asia Minor and Europa. Men sought better ways to live on earth, but negating the strong opinion of Mother Africa watching over them. Wary of prosecuting or ex-communicating defectors, kings and kingdoms sought the protection of other powers rather than Zenkepa. Man began to understand that what on earth was for the general good of mankind. Mother Africa liked that. It was her desire that man searches for ways leading to acquiring individuality. It would take man's independence away from her, but she wanted his devotion to be free to choose between her and what man created. She created special people that would fulfill man's wishes, leading the search for pieces of the puzzle from different parts of the earth who will seal all to fulfill the fullness of time.

As man put the pieces together, greed and ardent desire crept into giving way to the need for more. Famines and diseases resulted from their desire for more, as well as unemployment and crimes. Nether Zenkepa, nor its prayers, was able to help the sick, hungry, and impoverished. Breakaway kingdoms stool alone and, soon enough, its citizens began to explore the world in search of anything new that would make life worth living. Historians called this period the Great Discovery or Scramble.

More than forty countries planned to search the world for gods or goddesses, ideas, land, food, clothes, and anything to prove individual supremacy over their neighbors. Zenkepa remained a figurehead during these scrambles, receiving royalties from possessions, as well as donations, from its huge committed followers. Men revolutionized the paths to building huge industries, and needed more powerhouse for full production. The new land provided great prospect and profits to patronize science and technology (a new word for wizardry) and, the arts.

Notable amongst the great searchers were the city states of Eiffel, Big Ben and Bull, all related by blood and iron. Eiffel search was stopped due to internal wrangling, but maintained firmed grips on its discoveries. Bull classified himself as the center of the western world. Based on his viciousness, his devotion was searching dangerous terrain for land, food, clothes, and precious gems. More ambitious than most when he came to Fricano, he discovered the claws of the seven lion, a symbol of his cousin, proof that they had at one time passed through the region.

When Bull saw the army of well-built unemployed young people and healthy children playing in the Town Square, he proposed a solution of taking a batch of men to the new land beyond the wide sea for an experimental job. It seemed a good idea to the kings of several city states. This was how the first batch of Fricanoans sailed by ship to the new land; a project called racial cleansing and extermination. The point of the business plan was to fuel civil unrest, putting city states against each other. Citizens were gathered, captured, bought, and sold. Demand grew, opening several markets. People were put on shelves where city states, or an individual, could buy and owned as property. The race for profits and supremacy turned into an international conspiracy; punish the continent by dehumanizing it into a dark and deprive piece of land. While Bull and other city states were in the extermination business, and making profits, other aspiring city states crept in to share a piece of the pie.

This sickened the gods and they sent a message through the Oracle of Delphi;

> *'City states greed to fuel the industrial revolution*
> *for the creation of wealth will destroy the way of life*
> *of an entire group of people.'*

As for Big Ben, who was cunningly building battleships and

weapons of war, the new land was her pride possession. She called it Uncle Sam, a successful settlement program with new infrastructures and surpluses from cultivated soil. The race to Fricano proved a great success for Big Ben. She took in people along with their cultural possessions, lands and natural resources and made them her own. An enormous army put into place, subjects were tamed into obedience. Bull's power eventually began a decline, while Big Ben grew into a great power. Her army controlled and maintained peace within her empire, resulting in increased profits. She imposed increased taxes to gain more.

Men of freewill spoke out poetically; tension mounted. Once more, the gods spoke through the Oracle of Delphi;

'Love of weath, and nothing else, will ruin Big Ben.'

It wasn't long before Big Ben and Uncle Sam entered into full bloom confusion over a cup of tea. With Eiffel newly coined philosophy of butterfly wings and support, Uncle Sam opted for self-direction without hanging on the flicker of a satellite. In the end, Big Ben left defected.

Zenkepa never spoke against, or stopped, the sales of human. Donations from those countries engaged in selling human were accepted. Protecting its spiritual identity, Zenkepa buried its head.

Big Ben decided to free those from Fricano who fought alongside its army and were walking loosely in its bosom and protectorates. It contacted a guild to decide whether to integrate or return the Fricanoans back to their native lands. The latter was the accepted agenda, and a piece of land was negotiated along the renamed Coast of Guinea. The colony of Freetown was established. While Big Ben was resettling, its navy inspected ships which had fricanoans heading to the new world.

Uncle Sam also decided to follow suit, by freeing all Fricanoans who wanted to go back to the continent. Like Big Ben, Uncle Sam resettled returnees with the help of a society. The settlement was called Freeland, and capitol, named after its president. Freeland and Freetown became the pawns in the chess game between Big Ben and Uncle Sam.

As these settlements grew, Big Ben saw members of its colony seeking higher education for future leadership. Uncle Sam, on the other hand, after taking all Fricanoans to their side,

> 'This is your fatherland, explore its vast opportunity.
> I will purchase all that I can use.'

The Fricanoans who returned with less education, but street smart, shocked Uncle Sam with the news of progress, growth, and good governance amongst members of the colony. However, Uncle Sam did not accept, nor broadcast to the world the success of its pilot project. After all, it had been widely speculated that Fricanoans were sub-human and lacked the arts of governance. He rejected his own establishment, denied its existence and choked its improvements by withdrawing all support. Moreover, Big Ben and Effel were squeezing from the west, north and east, eating into Freeland. To survive, Freeland had to go on its own, declaring independence.

Big Ben recognized Freeland, irritating Uncle Sam.

CHAPTER SEVEN

The bright hall light showed twenty-four chairs in a V-formation, and two over-sized chairs placed to the left and the right side of the throne, forming a triangular. The pillars holding up the roof were invisible; the place, empty and cloudy. Then loud noise of people rushing echoed as six cats, six dogs, six cows and six goats took their place in the twenty-four chairs. Four human-like creatures sat opposite the animals, with the heads of a ram, lame bodies, hands on hips and elbows bent outward. They were all bowed legged and had a tail extending from their buttocks. These were special agents representing the four regions of the continent. Each region had four thousand demi-gods that carried out special assignments and messages to the other demi-gods in faraway lands. The four human-like creatures controlled a set of animal opposite the throne. A colossal figure sat on the throne, basically a gown without mortal structure. The figure wore a cone shape hat, but no head.

"Welcome to Kobamyou, the great hall in all of Africa," the figure on the throne greeted. "The combined forces of this world cannot dethrone us, and no problem would be left unsolved. What are your problems, gentlemen?"

One creature on the right stood, walked to the center of the triangular-shape formation, and bowed before the throne.

"Lord Tambo, your majesty," he said. "The western region brought a special message for us."

"Then say it, Pakamu," Lord Tambo ordered.

"Report from our switchboard has shown the ancient glory, the magnificent Falcon our forefather sought, has been given to the people of Liberia," Pakamu said. "We need that Falcon to increase our oil reserves and other minerals. Liberia could never be more important than Nigeria. They are not mature enough to handle such delicate gift of nature. The Falcon could be given to their so-called father."

"Thank you Pakamu," Lord Tambo said. "We saw the Falcon a thousand years ago in ancient Gougee. I disguised myself as a young man after a plot was made to destroy me. I lived in the northern region. I was there until Gougee was changed to Fricano and, remain there until it was captured and destroyed. We are only two magicians on earth now from the ancient world, Huntoe and me. Huntoe will never show himself to me because of what he and Koinyah did to the late Chief Kamauna and me."

"Lord Tambo, intelligence reports from one of our demi-gods in the north revealed that the Bokinabees are preparing to get the Falcon from Liberia," a creature called Blapa, declared. "Your majesty, this Huntoe, has planned that operation."

"Huntoe!" Lord Tambo exclaimed, sending baritone echo throughout the hall. "It's about time we see who has the greatest power. I've been looking for Huntoe all over this world, not knowing he's right next door. I could have gotten the seventh universal super power from Pampamyou, the highest institute of the mystical order, if the chief had lived. The power enables one to be present in one million places at the same time. And one would have supremacy over all forces. It enables you to give and take life.

"Gentlemen, I completed six thousand courses in magical arts at the Pampamyou traditional institute. This was the best magical institution the world has ever known below the Sahara. Huntoe is the product of that institute. It is time I dealt with that traitor, and bring the Falcon to Nigeria. We will attack Kjajuma in Burkina Faso, and our human agents will go to Liberia for the Falcon. As for you, Pakamu, you will have to attack the fortified most brilliant Fours and get their powers. In order to do this, you will visit the future city, Bozonboe, in the Forest of Fortune and Power for seven days."

"Remember this," Lord Tambo turned to Pakamu. "The fortified and most brilliant Fours are well respected in Nigeria. They have been on eight thousand missions and fulfilled all. These fox-looking creatures with human hands and legs can travel six thousand miles in a twinkle of an eye. They ended the Biafra war by spiritually disarming the fighters and defeated the Ozonma of Cameroon during the territorial dispute between Nigeria and Cameroon. Take your training seriously in this future city. Consider it a privilege to visit the future of mankind, but what you see there are all vanity. You are only there for weight control to aid you in the fight against the Fortified and brilliant fours."

"I will, my Lord," Pakamu assured him.

"Gentlemen, do we have any other thing to discuss?" Lord Tambo asked.

With no other business at hand, the meeting adjourn.

Pakamu reached the Forest of Fortune and Power entrance and chanted certain magical words. He stood and listened for a while, to see what would happen. Crickets chirping started faintly, and gradually changed to that of rushing water; then, swift-moving wind. He noticed the giant whirlwind head toward him. It immediately suctioned him to the innermost part of the forest; dense and cold. Then the wind carried him toward the sky, and begun to immediately descend into what seemed a boiling pot. There was no fire under the boiling pot into which Pakamu was plunged. He sank to the bottom, landing on a street paved with gold. A vehicle stopped.

"Welcome to Bozonbo, Pakamu," he heard a voice. "Welcome to the city of power and strength. You are in the Future; just see, but don't touch. Get in."

The car door opened and Pakamu entered.

Pakamu noticed the driver seat was empty. He fixed a face, holding his chin.

"Care for a drink?" A voice asked through the speakers.

"No, thanks," Pakamu said, looking around. "I'm okay."

Built like a spacecraft in full high technology, the interior of this vehicle called Fassace, was decorated in Kanti colors; red, gold and black. Designed to move on laser beams, it had no tires.

The vehicle took off and travelled throughout Bozonbo. Pakamu watched the people moving about on self-propelled devices.

"Like the people?" the voice asked.

"Yes, they are looking great."

"They eat once a week," the voice informed him. "Food is prepared with life-supporting nutrition to keep the inner organs young and alive."

Pakamu was amazed by this.

"It is now understood that once the inner organs are kept young and alive, human can live for several years," the voice continued. "Food is prepared with life supporting nutrition to keep the inner organs functioning. As they chewed, the food gives out a liquid-like substance, a substitute for water."

"Really?"

"In the open air, people can regulate the amount of breeze to blow and can scoop any amount of air, purify it and breathe in."

Pakamu nodded, taking all this in.

"We get our messages through the wind," said the voice.

"What about children? How do you start a family?"

"We have the opportunity of building the kind of family with your desire with a specific wife and have children. This is a complex combination of process called, Chromo-elevate."

"Chromo-elevate?"

"If you want a mate, wave your hand, and your bio-data appears. Then through an electro-synthesis, which is a connection between people, you directly affect another personality by molding a person to your wish."

"What about intercourse?" Pakamu asked.

"Because there is no distance between people, you can soul, or body, mate easily. Sleeping is by will; as one could control when, where, and how to sleep. You decide how long to live, and dying is a matter of option."

"My goodness!" Pakamu sighed.

"There's an incubator where you can separately host the

spirit and body of a person. If family members want a person to be brought back alive, the mechanism is easy. Aging is a matter of wish; a special body wash called, snake-medicato, provides the opportunity for a seventy-year-old to peel off his skin to an eighteen-year-old."

"How about your army?" Pakamu asked.

"We are the future," the voice said confidently. "Our infantry, or armed personnel, are not mandated to go to the Frontline. We fight through soul-travels and brain connection, hypnotizing the mind or brain file system. Through this means, one can deactivate the power within and control."

After a few turns, the vehicle entered a temple built in a gothic style. Six twenty-foot pillars held up the balcony of the temple. Four roof-like columns pointed into the sky, and thirty-five extra-large oval designed glass windows of different colors extended from the base of the roof to the top of the foundation. They stopped between the third pillar and the entrance to the great hall. The vehicle door opened and Pakamu got out.

"Welcome Pakamu," a great voice echoed from down the hall.

The monster, from which this voice came, was no different from Pakamu in structure. Only, it possessed human hands and feet, and a single eye on its forehead. The monster drew closer and chanted magical words that swept Pakamu off his feet. Pakamu somersaulted through an open hall and into a lake of fire.

"You will receive the twenty-ton power," the monster said. "This power will enable you to speak with any force and it will obey," the monster finished and walked away.

Pakamu spent forty-nine days in the forest, before returning to the Kolobamyou.

CHAPTER EIGHT

"There is something strange going on around here," Huntoe barked at his creatures. "Last night I saw, on our switchboard, four dangerous creatures from the southeast heading towards our kingdom. Where is Amioka the Great?"

"I am here, Master," the gigantic dog, with eagle claws and a lion's head, said as he entered the control room.

"Prepare for war!" Huntoe ordered.

"A war against the people of Liberia for the Falcon? That sounds good," Amoika declared.

"No, but strange creatures from Nigeria are heading our way with a plan to attack us," Huntoe corrected.

"Master," Yonkonda, Huntoe's information bird, entered the control room. "There is a powerful sorcerer in Nigeria called

Tambo," he informed. "I received information from my human agent that he is planning an attack against us."

"Tambo?" Huntoe shouted. "I've been trying to get him, and now he is mine. Amoika, get ready, we will attack!"

The great Amokika, whose body would be divided into six different creatures, was the most powerful creature in Burkina Faso. It is believed that this creature made Burkina Faso's land lack by sucking out the ocean and placing the country far away. Amoika turn the switch board on and saw three million demi-gods. These demi-gods he saw had heads of a peacock, bodies of a bat, and a long tail with an arrowhead at its end. Amoika rushed into the spirit world, dividing his body into three parts; each of his body parts had five hundred openings. One hundred and fifty spears, poisonous and explosive at each head, were sent out by Amoika. The demi-gods exploded and six hundred giant scorpions appeared; fortified and brilliant force.

The scorpion attacked Amioka from every direction. He fought fearlessly and noticed that their bodies were made of twelve-inch thick metal. Every spear that Amoika sent would bounce on the scorpion's bodies. Then the scorpions divided into sets of three, attacking each of Amoika's body part. Their tails projected secretion of glue-like liquid that cemented the openings. Amoika cleverly regrouped and transformed himself into hot lava. His body decomposed and vaporized, then rained upon the scorpions, burning them to ashes.

Pakamu appeared, turning into thick cloud, and rained on the lava.

Amoika disappeared, went above the cloud, and turned into a ball as mighty as the sun. He dried the water and rain cloud. Pakamu met him at the level of the heavens, and they begin insult attacks. Pakamu chanted magical words, turning Amioka into a bird, sending him towards the sun. Amoika, realizing the force carrying him, also chanted. Pakamu changed into a bat and went towards the sun as well. They continued their attacks as the forces carried both of them toward the sun. Pakamu flung the claw in his right wing into Amoika feathers, and Amoika pecked his beak deep into Pakamu's neck. They remain embedded in each other until the forces took them closer to the sun. There, they inevitably burned.

Huntoe jumped out of his seat, after seeing the destruction of Amioka. He assembled three thousand demi-gods and headed for Nigeria. Tambo quickly marshaled his host of demi-gods and went to meet Kjajuma, in the northern part of Ghana, a sacred province where spiritual battles are fought.

Huntoe reached the north and shouted at his demi-gods, turning them into a chain of mountains. Tambo shouted also, turning his demi-gods into snow, covering the chain of mountains. Then the two ancient rivals turned into their original selves. Huntoe waved his right hand and the sun stood still while Tambo waved and the moon appeared. Tambo commanded a million spears to attack Huntoe. The waving of Huntoe hands produced a million shields to block the spears. Huntoe stomped his right foot and the ground opened, taking Tambo slowly into the earth's crust. But Tambo swiftly commanded layers to appear under his feet as he was going down. The layers elongated, and like a springboard, brought him back to the earth's surface.

The opened areas cemented by itself. Tambo fluttered his right hand and cut Huntoe into two parts. Huntoe used his supernatural control to develop strings of nerves and joined the other half of his body. Tambo changed into a butterfly and flew away. Huntoe also turned into a dragonfly and chased after him. They met in the stratosphere and the insult attacks began all over.

An airplane flew by and sent them somersaulting to the earth in tiny pieces. The nose of the plane smashed in, causing a crash that took the lives of all the passengers. As Huntoe and Tambo died, their demi-gods melted, falling as dew.

CHAPTER NINE

Nagbe returned from work and his wife, Bleah, sat by his side as he ate his palm butter soup with rice.

"Bleah," Nagbe said, as soon as he finished chewing the last spoonful of rice. "My boss and I will be travelling to Voinjama tomorrow to attend a graduation ceremony of the Sande Society. About two hundred girls will be graduating from this traditional institute in different disciplines of womanhood. We will spend four days there. On our way back, we will stop in Gbarnga for two days to visit my boss's farm. Please take care of the house."

Bleah nodded to everything. Then, as if she'd just remembered something important, asked, "Why won't they stop this Sande initiation? The institution is good, but the innermost practice is dangerous to womanhood."

"Bleah," Nagbe said thoughtfully, "you'd better stop discussing things that could consume you. One cannot play with those people and their practice. They can get at you whenever you go against what they believe in... or can do in their shrine. I love you, and need you around."

He was smiling as he finished.

The next day Nagbe and his boss embarked on their journey to Lofa. Nagbe sat along side the driver in the passenger front seat while his boss sat in the back. The driver hummed to Sweet Mother, the popular song by Prince Nico, as it played on the radio. Soon they crossed the Fifteenth Gate near the Firestone Plantation Company, and Nagbe became uneasy. A chill went through his body, creating cold bumps on his skin. His body stiffened and sharp pains travelled from the soles of his feet up to the crown of his head. Nagbe grabbed his head and shifted it from side to side. He sat upright, and his mouth and eyes widely opened.

Simultaneously, the driver's eyes popped out of its sockets, as long rays of light encircled the boss' neck. The driver's body exploded from the back and his intestines oozed out and wrapped around his boss' body. The car moved from lane to lane, out of control. His natural reflexes created an attempt to press on the brake pedal; it did not hold. The car ran off the road and into the dish, killing the driver and Nagbe's boss. Critically wounded, Nagbe was taken to Du Side Hospital.

Four wizards from Nigeria appeared on the scene.

"The Falcon can now be taken to Nigeria," one said cheerfully. "Let's go and get the Falcon, as you can see, they are dead."

Two weeks later, the driver, as well as Nabge's boss, was buried at the Palm Grove cemetery. An array of government officers attended this sad occasion. After the funeral, a group of women accompanied Bleah to their residence, and later to the Du Side Hospital.

Five wizards from Bokina Faso entered the Nagbes home as soon as Bleah had left. They searched the house and located the Falcon wrapped in a blanket, hidden in a kitchen cupboard. A bright light from the Falcon filled the room when they unveiled it. Shades of blues, greens, yellow and red lights dangled over the Falcon. This fascinated the wizards, they began dancing and singing their national anthem. A red light brightened and a drum sounded. The wizards stopped immediately.

The beat from the Falcon increased its pitch and produced good juju music. A force swept the wizards off their feet and made them to dance. They danced to heavy pace, looking like a whirlwind in motion. Then the wizards stuck together and passed through the window and into the streets, sweeping plastic bags, paper, dust and dry leaves, which ended in the Montserrado River.

The light went off on the Falcon.

The Nigerians entered. The light came on again, and they went back outside. They had been instructed by Tambo that whenever they saw that particular ray of light, then the Falcon was in its dangerous mood. The wizards changed themselves to Nagbe, Bleah, and Nagbe's boss and entered the house. They collected the Falcon, wrapped it in a blanket and went outside. The wizards got into a car and drove down Lynch Street, made a bend on United Nations Drive and headed for Bassa Community. There was a traffic jam toward Bassa Community, so they took the by-pass in front of the Police Headquarters. As their Land Rover passed the station, a police officer recognized the already dead minister, and pursued the jeep. The police car made a U-turn, turn on the siren and followed the Land Rover. The police vehicle caught up in front of the University of Liberia, and slightly crossed in front of it. The officer got out and walked to the Land Rover. To his surprised, there were four Nigerians dressed in their native gown seated in the car.

"Officer, what is the matter?" one passenger asked.

"I am sorry, Sir," the officer apologized, staring at the passengers. "I was chasing a similar vehicle," he said. Giving no other explanation, he walked away.

The Falcon sensed it was in the wrong hands. It jumped out of the blanket like jack-in-the-box and flew above the Nigerians. However, it stuck on the car ceiling, and red light shot in every direction. Smoke cloud entered the mouths of the Nigerians, sealing it. The Falcon then turned hot and exploded, sending the car aflame. Twenty-four thousand demons spread into the open air, accompanied by four beautiful girls wearing silk gowns. The first girl, Azone's, gown was red, and on a plate hanging from her neck read, Queen of Sickness. She commanded her portion of demi-gods and they went into the open air. Bladja, the second girl, Queen of Destruction, commanded her portion of demi-gods to enter every statue in the country. The third girl, Calven, Queen of Strange Happening, sent her demi-gods to infect every body of water. Dolwa, the fourth girl, Queen for the Pollution of the Earth, instructed her demi-gods to enter the earth.

Azone turned four thousand insects into beautiful girls who entered the human population in various cities to infect young men with deadly diseases. Bladja turned five thousand demi-gods into young men and women who posted as doctors and nurses in various hospitals, clinics, drug stores and marketplaces. She also instructed several insects to make different kinds of curative drugs and made several others to be outdated. These drugs, cheaply sold, pushed aside genuine medical supplies and drugs.

Calven ordered her demi-gods to pull people into the water. Some bodies had bullet holes or burnt. Dolwa's demi-gods pulled out every mineral and crop, invited con artists and looters who signed bogus contracts to exploit the country. She established men of lower status and placed them into positions of trust, only to steal and not to improve the country. They sought juju to settle misunderstanding. Many people died in the event. Fears galloped over the country, incompetent people relied on juju to stay in power, as well as to protect their position. She also changed hummingbirds into pastors who only preached for the offerings.

Two months after, people were dying in the streets, and many were displaced. A strange disease entered Monrovia, killing people in opened places. The disease also caught people who were under the first round of rainfalls at the end of the rainy season. Others caught the disease through close contact; thus, many avoided public places and most stay home. Companies put many employees on compulsory leaves. Business men went out of goods due to the closures of the ports of entry. Prices rose, street vendors went out of business and unemployed youths roamed the streets.

The economy broke down and the Liberian dollar climbed to the exchange rate of hundred-fifty to one United States Dollar. Due to the deteriorating nature of the situation, friendly nations sent tons of relief food items to Liberia, to save the people from starvation. Other nations turned their back on the country and closed their borders. Planes and ships stop traveling to Liberia. Foreign nationals, including business people and investors, began leaving the country. Liberia was now considered a failed state and declared as the most unsafe and unstable country south of the Sahara.

The president declared a state of emergency. Citizens and cabinet meetings were called for a strategic plan to curb the situation. The citizens, through a spokesperson, gave their support to the government, and promised to back the government on whatever measure it wished to take. At the cabinet meeting, the Minister of Local Government, after several convincing acts of rhetoric, told the government to call all the Zoes in the country to help fight the strange happening. Christians organized crusades and religious activities to contain the situation, they rebuked the minister for his pronouncement. The government didn't listen, but organized a Zoes conference.

Zoes from the various counties converged in Monrovia and decided to merge as a giant force, headed by old man Zubah Torwala, to go into their shrines for one week.

The Zoes consulted their juju and went on national and local radio stations instructing the citizenry to sacrifice six white chickens, cook enormous quantities of white rice, add red palm oil, six white kola nuts, and place the rice at every intersection in the country. Several persons performed the sacrifice.

Thereafter, relative calm returned to the country. The Zoes were conferred with the highest honor at the city hall and given envelopes containing money. The Zoes recommended that the legislative body passes into law that the secrets of juju be taught in schools. Every government official was to enter the highest order of mystical secret society, and every citizen be mandated to enter the Sande and Poro secret societies. Women group protested, due to the danger certain aspect of the initiation posed to a woman's well-being. They called for reformed. Several persons and communities protested against the bill, the legislative body passed the bill anyhow, based on the president's recommendation.

The demi-gods regrouped after three months and came back with a most terrifying force. Chief Zoe Torwala saw the demi-gods through the spiritual lenses and announced on state radio that a strange plague was going to hit Liberia; everybody, big or small, was to hang an animal bone around his or her neck as a way out. All Christians refused. Things became worse as people were abducted and never found.

People became frustrated because of the high rate of unemployment. Armed robbery was on the rise, and the government did nothing about it. Teenagers plunged into prostitution to beat the system, and other crime rate increased. Men were marrying men. Sexual exploitation became the gateway to getting a job and getting out of school. Liberians were now going back to refugee camps, while college graduates could not prove what they learned at job sites. Fake degree holders entered the country from all regions of Africa and terminated the contracts of those who questioned them. Those observed to be incompetent reverted to juju to maintain their positions. Neegee society resurfaced, and people were mysteriously found dead in the waters. Lebanese merchants closed their stores and left the country, quickly turning Liberia into a ghost town.

CHAPTER TEN

Cunnuka was more than a worshipful place. Its population had increased over the years with souls possessing various competence. The province was the size of the Delta State in Nigeria. The buildings were about the size and height of the pyramid of Giza in Egypt. They were in rows of three with twenty-seven in each block. The place was the main dwelling of Mother Supreme and her hosts of attendants and armies. Surrounding Mother Supreme was the Seventh Council of Elders of Africa. They discussed issues affecting the continent at a round table.

In the north of Cunnuka is the town called, Toukongo, the intellectual town, where all the fallen heroes and heroines of Africa live. This town of arts and cultures, fora and intellectual discourses, had a great Palava Hut called, the Hut of Zenu, where issues ranging from philosophy, economics, and politics among others were discussed. Toukongo was about the size of Monrovia and had no government. The act of governance was most times considered evil, as the governors would fashion good behavior into attitudes that promoted self-centeredness and created disunity. Individuals were considered more educated to be governed by someone else.

A poet named Zulu Menya, wrote a poem and it was at the center of discussion in the hut of Zenu. Zulu Menya was rich in verse, had a wealth of experience, and an independent orator whose influence would be felt throughout the length and breadth of Cunnuka. The poet stood before the audience of great men and read his poem entitled, 'That Earth';

"O Earth,
That land of fallen angels and crazy gods;
What more will you take?
Who are the sinners and who are the saints?
Did Jesus Christ die a saint or a sinner?
Did Mohammed die a saint or a sinner?
Maybe Niccolo Machiavelli,
Or Mohammed is the saint, and Jesus is the sinner.
The might of the saints have over-ruled the morality
of the sinners.
The acts of the saint are said to justify the weakness
of the sinners.
O Earth,
That land of disgrace,
What have you done?
Who are the good people and who are the bad
people?
The good people rule the earth.
Those who opposed the good people are the bad
people.
Bad people can become good people
If they befriend the good people.
That earth is a mess."

Zulu Menya concluded and looked around. Martin Luther King, Jr., Steve Beko, Edward Wilmot Bladen, Saka Zulu, Harriet Tubman, Malcolm Little (Malcolm X), Marcus Garvey, George Washington Carver, and many other heroes and heroines were in the audience. Joseph Jenkins Roberts, Africa's first President, served as moderator. Martin Luther King, Jr. buttressed the poet's view of the earth, being a place infected with more wicked people.

"The great Mother Supreme created a haven," King said. "But the haven has been turned into a self-styled paradise by some good people who derive happiness through rough means. All mankind needs to do is to 'turn the left ear.'"

As King concluded, the main entrance to the hall opened. Everyone turned to find the senior spokesperson for Mother Supreme, and foreign residence for information on every town, entered the hall. Per protocol, Joseph Jenkins Roberts announced the arrival of Klap, who was immediately taken to the podium by the great escort, Marcus Garvey.

"Ladies and gentlemen, men of honor and power, intellectuals," Klap began. "I am sent by Mother Supreme to inform you of the mayhem on earth; to be particular, that small Negro republic, Liberia. The Falcon, sent by Sister Congo, daughter of Arka and Zula, to help the country, could not succeed because the chosen one could not get it to its destination. Nigeria and Mali were in Liberia for this supernatural entity. The Falcon is capable of pulling resources from everywhere to improve the living standard of its citizens and national development. It has the potentials to increase a man's love and trust for his country, enabling him to increase his thinking faculties to the highest level of understanding. Nigeria got it, but the Falcon refused and exploded, causing many problems for the inhabitants."

"Liberia," Zulu Menya interrupted, "that insignificant country, is soaked in the vortex of its sins. The justice system has been destroyed by Masonic craft, the economy, undermined and overtaken by rogues. The social and moral means are operated by self-proclaimed gods, sycophants and hypocrites. The code of justice, 'Innocent until proven guilty' has been turned into 'guilty until proven innocent'. The citizenry is vain-looking and struggling for identity. Their cultures are far retched.

"What cannot happen there?" Zulu Menya went on. "Babylon is now a harlot, a blood thirsty viper which surfaced in churches, companies, government, and everywhere. Who's there to ask a self-administered country, and its groups of misdirected people, a generation of vipers? The love of self is the greatest evil that has conquered that nation. The attitude of the majority of its citizenry puzzles one and yet, they claim to be civilized. The American way of civilization in someway, somehow, to Christianize the continent through the establishment of that country, has altered an entire way of life of the aborigines. Yet, no one holds them responsible for such evil. Everyone does what he wants by his own standard. Like a proverbial ostrich, the so-called role models, bury their heads. Liberia still doesn't have a tonic to drink for self-awareness and self-reliance."

"How dare you speak evil of that glorious land of liberty," snapped Marcus Garvey. "She is a member of the United Nations… a stepchild of the United States."

"Marcus, didn't you hear what Bismarck said," Zulu Menya asked. "'There is no altruism amongst nations. The strong shall rule the weak with 'blood and iron'. United Nations," he said the name with disgust. "The same line separating the rich and poor runs through the two categories of nations. How many nations decide the fate of the world? Is it the block of the real politics or the block of the stick and carrot? Does the United Nations stands in the middle or leaning? Will the majority ever rule the few? No matter how long the majority will stay picking, the minority will always make decisions and lead the majority. Again, I am asking... Will the majority ever lead the few?"

When no one responded, Zulu Menya answered, "No. It is a far fetched reality. Where was the United Nations when many people were killed in Rwanda and other places? Patrick Lumumba, where was the United Nations? Samuel Kenyon Doe, where was ECOMOG? Maybe the United Nations can only make a lot of money when disasters strike a nation and its people. This United Nations, I believe, is a football game among five brothers who came out of a single mother, and contesting in a league where one has absolute supremacy, or weighs the so-called balance of power. Look at my brother Tolbert, before his death, he was the chair of the OAU, did he do good or bad? Liberia, why are you such a weakling? What happened to your birthright? Why did you sell it to the United States, your father?

"Liberia was at the founding of the League of Nations and the United Nations; all along, who side did she lean on? You guess! This is why that country has been treated like a dog, wagging its tail at the master's table.

"United Nations? Are nations truly united? United for what? Against whom? Who is regulating? Who's influencing? If united, why are they still fussing and fighting about supremacy, about trade and commence? About who has the biggest alum of weapons? About ideologies, etc. If united, why aren't there across the board mandated standard for all nations in trade, education, societal standard, etc.

"Perhaps we must rethink the role of the 'United Nations' in handling the affairs of all nations. A stepchild of the United States? Ha, ha, ha," Zulu laughed.

"The United States has never loved that country, and prayed never to associate itself with that country or its inhabitants. It created a country out of fears and lies, putting the chiefs at gunpoint, got a land and dashed its unwanted people there. The US turned its back on its citizens, hoping they would die in the wild. But it went in search of friends and children-Phillipines (a special relationship), Taiwan, South Korea, etc.

"But Liberia has never experienced such special relationship; maybe it's the color of their skin or being their former slaves. The country has always been there for the US, and if the United States wants Liberia to be developed, it will be developed. If the United States wants corruption to stop in Liberia, it will stop. Just about anything the US wants to happen in Liberia, or wants Liberia to do, it will surely do; even at the detriment of its citizens.

"Did you not see how the United States asked Liberia's president to step down, and he did it? If the US wants the strange happening in Liberia to end today, it will surely end. They are still the US outcast, and the US has been blinded by the reality that a 'slave and master' cannot sit at the same table," Zulu finished with a broad smile.

William V.S. Tubman said to Zulu Menya, "This is not the issues at the United Nations or the US."

"Tubman," Zulu Menya replied, dropping the pitch of his voice. Then he walked over and stood by Klap. "Let me tell you something about a writer who wrote a play called, Open-close

Connections, just to glorify his master," he said. "The actor, Tollack, had a tragic end because he saw the flaws in his so-called policies of growth, unity and identity. That writer became his creator's greatest puppet, and his love for pleasure provided growth without development. I wish the creator of Liberia had told Joseph, and other leaders, that a divided house ends up in carious. During the economic boom, Liberia's father rushed into the country to exploit because he knew the country Achilles' heels; poverty, vulnerability, ardent affection, and dependence."

"Menya," A. Doris Banks Henries exclaimed, "Stop politicking this situation. We need to find a way to help."

"Yes, I will stop," Zulu Menya said. "We will find a way to help Liberia. Camara Laye, would you please come closer."

Camara came and stood by Zulu.

"As a skillful writer, I know you can write a good story about us in Toukongo," Zulu Menya said. "I may not master the craft, but do we only write history for the minority? Most time I asked myself when reading Liberian history, 'who were Long peters, Boatswain? How did Firestone build a dam to boost its operations? How did it recruit its workforce to build the dam and what was their condition? Who was Matilda Newport? Why is she being idolized and monument standing on the grounds of the Centennial Pavilion? A school named in her honor? I believe she was great, but what are the moral restitutes behind her greatness? Who was Bob Gray? Why weren't we told that the Provenance Baptist, in which the Liberia's Declaration of Independence was signed, was built directly on the site of the most honored Mamba's traditional society shrine? Do we know Wannie Gbotoe, Liberia's greatest footballer? What was his story? Do we know why that piece of land was called Sinkor? Do we know why? I believe history must tell us why, this is why.

"I still want to know, Camera," Zulu Menya continued. "Are there any virtues in literature and the arts, or creativity, in Liberia? Do we know about R. Vanjah Richards, Ti-Consay Roberts, Morris Dorley, Bai T. Moore, Albert Porte, Caesar Gartor, to name a few. I know their contributions are like passing memories. Would Miatta Fahnbulleh, Hawa Daisy Moore, Michael Francis, George Weah, Zaye Tete, Fatu Gayflor, Kenneth Best, and others, whose talents are shaping positive image of the country on the local and international scene, ever be remembered like their predecessors? Where does the country stand as there are no role models or heroes?

"Liberia, why don't you make your so-called creator, the United States, shame? If my father abandoned me, I will tell him in his face or reject him publicly. If he wants my talents, he will not get it on discount or privilege. Liberia needs to show, like the days of first, second and third president, its creator that it can make it on its own without waiting for handout or subsidies.

"Liberia, it's time to wake up, unshackle, and limit all ties with your creator; except trade, commerce and mutual respect, and develop into a better outcast. Liberians need to respect, love God, and care for their country and fellow man. The country is indeed a paradise to adore.

"Martin," he turned to Dr. King. "Why can't black people remember, during the celebration of black history month, those gallant men who braved the storm and travelled to Africa and establish a country which led the way for all other African nations?"

"Zulu Menya, this is enough," Klap appealed.

The poet nodded and walked to his seat. Dweho Tweh commended him.

"Mother Supreme will need a solution," Klap continued. "And a plan in handling the situation in Liberia within seventy-two hours."

Thomas Sankara stood, cleverly positioned his red beret and said, "I suggest we send Patmoonyan, Africa's best detective, and some African heroes."

"Thomas, the idea is brilliant," Edwin J. Barclay said. "I can see again, the bodies of Patrick Lumunba and Samuel Doe in a pool of blood before the eyes of the so-called heroes."

"Why don't we send an unknown person," Felix Houphoet Boigny suggested. "Liberia needs peace, and the survival of my country depends on that peace."

"The security of my country also depends on peace in Liberia," Shaka Stevens added. "This was the reason we established the Mano River Union. Am I not right, Ahmed Sekou Toure?"

"Ahmed, Felix and Shaka, do you still have in your possession pieces of land belonging to Liberia," Zulu Menya asked. "At that time, your masters bullied Liberia and ceased those lands. Right?"

"Yes," Shaka replied. "Liberia cannot manage a diamond field or a Gola Forest. I met the arrangement, and no one can blame me."

"Indeed," Ahmed confirmed. "I met it as it was. But they never asked for it."

"Yes," Felix answered, "but I met the arrangement. Liberia cannot manage the other land in her possession. What can it do with land from Dananee downward, San Pedro and a little strip of land along the border? They don't care because they never asked for it. I don't believe they have the capacity."

"Whatever reason you think is best, one day Liberia will request for those pieces of land," Zulu Menya declared. "In the spirit of brotherhood, be prepared to return the land to save the cordial relationship, or is there need to show a clear boundary between Liberia and Sierra Leone, Guinea and Liberia, and Ivory Coast and Liberia."

"Dr. King and Malcolm," Zulu went on, pointing at both men, "Once the history of Liberia is not remembered, or considered, as a tributary to the continued struggle for civil rights of Africans in the United States, their story is incomplete. Depict a disservice to those gallant men who left the United States to go back to the land of their ancestors to prove that black people were capable of governance, history showed that they made it in the mist of nothing. However, Washington refused to recognize their greatness.

"But Liberia has been long forgotten by African-Americans, although its constitution provides rooms for citizenship for those of African descent, and forbids white men from being citizens. Why? Because black people were denied civil rights in the United States, a place where their sweat and blood never appreciated or recognized throughout its growth and development processes. It is a payback for all African-Americans. Therefore, African-Americans need to appreciate Liberia, and to invest in its vast resources and make the land a paradise of hope to forfeit the dreams of its founding fathers. Liberia was also a haven for Stokely, Nina, and others who wanted support in their quests for freedom. It leadership never turned away anyone and even provided traveling documents.

"Where is Marcus Garvey?" Zulu Menya asked, looking around.

"I am right here," Garvey answered and stood.

"Please, sit, sir," Zulu motioned him. "I want to thank you for the Back to Africa Movement. In this dispensation, it can still work. Let all blacks, without direct African connections, rushed for the 'All-Africans Spiritual Connection' by getting husbands or wives from Africa. Their children will have a home in Africa. Because of their children, they could make it their home too. It is also time for the Black Movement to put the continent on their agenda; advocating for social justice, economic and social involvement of all citizens, strengthening cultures. And, bring to book, through advocacies, all dishonest and unscrupulous leadership."

Loud laughter erupted at this proposal.

"It's time for business," Zulu declared. "Everyone is to propose a decision with a need to understand Liberia's problem. We must dig deeper into its root causes. I've been following history of that country and have put together a documentary that may shape our final decisions."

Everyone nodded in agreement of what Zulu Menya had suggested.

"I hate Liberia for its stupidity and dependance," Zulu Menya added, "But, I love that country and its people and was happy to hear that a young professional program made of brilliant young men, are being mentored to take over the affairs of government. Most conservatives will not like the idea. They might even want to use the 'Kill them before they grow' strategy. But a private-public agreement protecting Liberia's honest and finest, will save the country.

"Those young professionals are vital to any proposal of taking Liberia to another level. With proper training, they could be used as specialists and principle officers void of political interferences. I also believe that in order for reform and development to strife in Liberia, the issues of governance and growth must not be an object just for politicians or the economists. It must be looked at from the lenses of all artists, economists, poets, scriptures, politicians, and others, to form a common component and Liberia as the subject."

CHAPTER ELEVEN

The two-hundred-fifty inch television, built into the wall to screen or project image during the discussion, was turned on. Zulu Menya began his documentary in this fashion;

'So she said to Abraham, cast out this slave woman with her son, for the son of this slave woman shall not be an heir with my son Isaac.'

"From this passage in the Bible, Liberia's trouble started," Zulu said. "If your mother is, or was, a slave, who then are you? With a few loaves of bread and a few gallons of water, a certain amount of Fricanos was cast out of the house of their owners and sent back to the land of their ancestors. Their journeys began with a lie, and they settled on the land of other people with the same kind of lie. Therefore, lies created Liberia, and lies destroyed Liberia.

"There were successes and failure, death and conflicts, even regrets due to rejection. The constant lookout for a wealthy father who may pass by to drop bread crumbs from his table and show the world that his father in some way, somehow, cared for his outcast son. In the land of their ancestors, although strange, Uncle Sam outcasts began a story that is of pity and neglect, of bullying and frustration, mistakes and double standard, greed and loneliness, poverty in the mist of plenty; but indoctrinated to seek for humanitarian aid and, the psychology of fatherly pretense and lies, making the proclamation of self direction became the final results.

"Their settlement became known as Liberia. I will now show you the chronology of notable eras of some of the events of the ills, and so-called 'good' the father had done to his bastard against what the bastard has done for his camaleone father.

"In 1822, Uncle Sam Congress approved $100,000 for Elizabeth to sail to Africa. This is the beginning of our investigation. Yet, Uncle Sam refused to acknowledge that it created a nation, and colonized a group of people. When asked, he will blame it on an NGO, the American Colonization Society. Can an NGO of a particular country established and colonized a nation? It is not true, but let me not deviate. Let us first look at the outcast's demonstration of love for his so-called Uncle Sam.

"The love of his father prompted Liberia to change the name of its capital city from the name of Jesus Christ, Christopolis, to the name of the President of Uncle Sam. Liberia kept a star it took from Uncle Sam, and placed it in its flag; hoping his father will consider his rejection and the return will be an easy integration.

Its constitution was modeled after his father, and system of governance model after him too. Its preamble, culture, language, just everything, was done either less or more closer to its father's. The country was meant to be the complete replica of its father, with the little dots of an inhumane act of the Fernando Po case and a stratified society. Let's look at possible intervention from Uncle Sam that could spur growth and development in Liberia," Zulu Menya encouraged.

Everyone remained attentive.

"Before 1860, the prospect of Liberia being a great agricultural country was visible to the entire world," Zulu Menya continued. "It would have proven that indeed freed slave have the brain to handle a country from nowhere, to a great economic power on the so-called Dark Continent. But, its father did not provide the outcast with an industrial based. Besides, the training of the settlers in the art of financial management, specialized training for accountability, would have been a huge success. Great Britain knew this and accepted several members of the Mende and other tribes into special universities in London. Sadly, an all-American born and educated cabinet under Joseph Roberts and other presidents, could not, or may not, make a difference. They failed miserably to provide the right skills, or leadership to take a tiny little country from poverty to a great economic power on the continent of Africa. It is disappointing.

"Anyhow, the settlers made a country like their father and, like their father, they experienced many skirmishes with the original owners of the land. If a certain group of people with different identity than those they met are living together, but separated by a long line, there will be confusion. Everyone may fight to protect, maintain, or secure their way of life from being contaminated. If

Uncle Sam truly wanted to be associated with this country called Liberia, it could have influenced a policy decision to integrate the group of people they met. But this was not the case. Like Uncle Sam, they fought their way through those they met-a circle.

"Gentlemen, because of the ineptness of its father in raising a child, Liberia experienced killing and looting, self destruction and hatred couple with international conspiracy; all became the back blast from neglect, an uneven integration and immature strife for independence. The quest for financial stability forced Liberia into getting the death, financial and economic dependency loans from Great Britain and United States, its own father. E. J. Royce, would you kindly tell us what happened?"

"I like to reserve my comments," Royce replied.

The audience erupted with murmurs.

Zulu Menya waited for the murmurs to grow quiet before continuing.

"But Uncle Sam, afraid of responsibility, has always been pretending to be a good man going to other nations and providing handouts," he said. "At home, he never mentioned to his other children, grandchildren and great-grandchildren, about his bastard. He made sure to keep the secret in a way that his offspring will never believe that their father fathered a child who is living in Africa. The state of Virginia is honest enough to remember Liberia by dedicating an avenue. But whenever a father rejects, or abandons, a child, there will always be one who will stick like a brother. That country was Germany.

"The Germans made it their duty to trade with Liberia as a major trading partner, and gave its government a sense of control and pride. Liberia's economy was picking up. But how did Liberia pay back the Germans? Neglect. To appease a father who had rejected and abandoned it during difficult times, and how it had been told by Big Ben and Eifel, that the Germans' presence in Liberia was unacceptable. Liberia declared war on Germany during World War I. The gods wept on how the Germans were forced out of Liberia and how their properties looted. The German war ship had to calm down the disappointed Germans by shelling Monrovia. Liberia did not know that that decision was a planned tactic by its father to sabotage its recovering economy.

"This mistake by Liberia crippled the country's economy, which was later made worst by the great depression of the 20s. Liberia had to again go begging for money in the early 1920s. Like a child, although an outcast, Liberia went crawling to its father. The Liberians begged from March to October until a loan of five million dollars was approved by the White House; but Congress did not concord. The hope of the Liberians was dashed until a private citizen, a son of its father who became a businessman, knew that there was need to compete with Great Britain as the automobile industry was booming. His brother was desperate for money (he had the right temperature for the planting of rubber) because their father had turned him down. As the old proverb says, 'a drowning man will hang on to anything,' made the delegation to take a loan of five million dollars from their brother for a forty-year period to settle all outstanding loans with Great Britain and the United States, its own father who had denied him the same sum of money.

"In Liberia, it is called 'digging a hole to cover a hole'. The loan was for one million acres of land for ninety nine years, at an annual rate of six cents per acre; any diamond, gold, silver, oil, and any other minerals found on the land, were for his brother. In the presence of their father who was not blind, Jacob took away Esau birth right."

This aggravated Malcolm X, who stood up and angrily said, "This is crazy. Who owes who?"

"To put it simply," Zulu Menya said, "I took five million from you for a long period, at a cheaper rate; then I gave you land and mineral rights. Do I have to pay you back? Did his brother pay taxes? Where is Tubman? Barclay, where were you guys?"

No one said a word; Tubman and Barclay sat with their heads hung.

"I did what I could have done," Tolbert spoke out. "Posterity knows that, but I became the bad guy."

"Yes," Tubman cut in, "a 'bad guy' for nepotism!"

"You can say that, Tubman," Tolbert said, incredulously. "Because of your inept, you mortgaged the country to foreigners."

The two men exchanged disagreement for a while.

"Stop!" Malcolm X yelled. "Stop acting like children."

The men discontinued.

"Go on, Zulu," Malcolm X encouraged, then took his seat.

"Liberia's father's son's company shocked the world with its forced recruitment policy," Zulu Menya continued. "He indirectly administered the affairs of the country. Firestone directly and indirectly ruled Liberia, becoming a country in a country.

"During World War II, Liberia offered its land free of charge to his father to build the needed facilities to fight the axis forces, and combat the spread of communism throughout Africa. Liberia was now the land for hosting and refueling it father's military aircraft. The landing base was situated near its father's son's rubber plantation. This time around, the father provided financial aid, and a drive through by the then president, rekindle, as the Liberians believe, father-son-relationship. From 1962 to the end of the first republic, Uncle Sam military and economic aid to his outcast was close to three hundred million dollars, according to several history books. What did his father get in return," Zulu Menya asked.

The audience sat mute.

"I will tell you," Menya continued. "His father built a spying station called the Omega Tower to handle intelligence traffics, and built a relay station to boost its propaganda arm of its broadcast channel to the rest of the world. Then Liberia became it father's puppet at the United Nations and other gatherings; even spying on other countries during the Organization of African Unity meetings. But Liberia was in a difficult position; fighting for grips into its political and economic quest, advocating for an independent Africa, and appeasing its father.

"Do you wonder why Liberia has never been seen as the greatest defender and promoter of Africa right to independence? When all countries in Africa were still under colonial rules, Liberia was the one and only voice for Ghana, Nigeria, Sierra Leone, South Africa, Kenya, and others. Their freedom fighters visited its presidency for guidance and financial supports; looking up to Liberia to propagate its voice for Africa's independence at the League of Nations, the United Nations, and other international organizations. Some African freedom fighters were given Liberian Passports to travel around the world.

"Is Liberia being remembered as a hero, or a coward, and puppet or as Anti-Pan Africanism? They forgot that at that time, Liberia was not the only so-called independent country; Ethiopia was. Wasn't Ethiopia an Uncle Sam puppet? But Ethiopia is still being praised and honored. Does the African Union remember, or recognize Liberia's contribution to Pan-Africanism, African Unity or being the lone voice in African nation's desire for freedom from the colonial masters? Or, is Liberia being punished because of her father? Maybe the country has not the mantle to market to the world its contributions to Africa freedom and liberation. Nowadays, nobody remembered Sanniquelle in Liberia, and what that little town did for African Unity. Liberia needs to wake up, because it has done a lot. Who has stolen the show for Pan-Africanism? I will surely leave that to your conscience."

Jomo Kenyatta said, "I still believe that Liberians are not marketing their contributions to the freedom of the African continent, for instance, the African Development Bank."

"But Liberia, the outcast and underdog," Zulu said, smiling, "is still unworthy of its father's trust. Liberia lack of financial management and financial management specialist; plus measurable tools for accountability, created a living, but dead, country. Its weakness was exploited instead of being strengthened by its father, Big Ben, and Eifel.

"Liberia also deposed trade partners with the Germans. From 1904 to 1912, Liberia was still a debt-shackle country; an 1871 debt with the balance of $800,000 still hanging around its neck, and another $500,000 from the Briton. This is written in the great-grand history books, and there were mounting calls for development which involved extending into the interior. Its only option was to run to those with the big bucks; its father, whom it has always called Uncle Sam, Big Ben, and other nations for a loan.

"For Uncle Sam, Big Ben, the Germans, Eifel, and the Dutchman, to co-signed and make available a loan of $1.7 million, (with conditions), Liberia had to give up part of its independence by allowing her father to appoint a master receiver of all monies, and place a person at the head of its revenue collection posts, which was mostly custom duties.

"The Oracle of Delphi told the gods that in the future, Liberia would face the same control system, but in a slightly different way. This internationally acknowledged head of the Liberian treasury, used 40% of the collected revenue annually to pay the debts owed Uncle Sam. Employees of the custom department, and the militia, used their power to beat, maimed, tortured, and killed those who refused to pay, or those who never had the means to pay, the hut tax. Those who never had the means to pay had to send their children as pawns to people living along the coast, working under any conditions, just to enable their parents to make these payments. Due to its success and individual interest, Big Ben, Eifel and the Germans, also appointed and assigned revenue collectors at the treasury to collect money for repayment of debts."

"Interesting," Jomo Kenyatta declared.

"Yes, Jomo," Zulu Menya acknowledged. "Big Ben had the largest chunk of debt, and it was glaring that Liberia would become maritime giants, making a lot more money. The Germans ships were very frequent. To prevent the German ships from the grips of Big Ben and Eifel and others, the Germans needed someone at the port of entry as pseudo-agent to collect what was termed, German debt. But the Germans were later cut off when World War I started. With the others still around, Liberia was an international holding, or trustee, where every country, it owed, had its currency as a national purchasing power. Consequently, Big Ben really wanted a complete takeover as she appointed an additional revenue collector, and requested that a Briton be head of the national militia, which were using all manner of means to attract taxes from the majority of the people who were not represented in the government; but with sweat and blood, had to pay taxes. Who was paying the Briton? That is still a mystery."

The audience gasped.

CHAPTER TWELVE

"In the beginning, Barclay needed the equivalence of $500,000," Zulu Menya continued. "Since he could not get it from the country's fathers, like 1871, he decided to also seek it from Big Ben. Big Ben agreed, but not like country to country; except through a British company and a Liberian company. The British designed the plan and the strategy. Johnston had to take full responsibility of the loan, and serve as the chair of a British company, which the government had to lie to the public; that it was a Liberian with exclusive rights to construct roads, and communication networks in Monrovia and Harper. He would have the rights to prospecting for minerals and exploiting all, leasing of land, and for fisheries and guaranteeing of loans. The company had the right to establish a police force to protect its properties. The company became a government within a government.

"Like the Liberian Development Company, Ltd, other companies which later went to Liberia had been granted or requested for similar privileges. While the company was on holiday, getting richer through privileges and rights, the Liberian government was struggling to pay an annual amount of £30,000 as interest until the loan was repaid. Additional two Britons were brought in and put in charge of the custom revenue, as well as serving as security to the British financiers. The British Bank of West Africa, stationed in Sierra Leone, was the custodian of all the collected revenue. It is written that a monthly allowance of $9,000 was remitted to Monrovia for government operating expenses. Who knows how much was collected by the British? Who was assigned as Liberia personnel to verify, or counter check, what the Britons were actually receiving?"

"How did you get all this information?" Thomas Sankara asked.

"It is written in all textbooks," Zulu Menya answered. "It's an opened secret. My brother, if you search you will see a lot more sickening tales than what I am telling you. And, Thomas, it is regrettable that that company, the Liberian Development Company, Ltd, did not fulfill all of its obligations. It constructed a fifteen-mile road, and a gravel road along the St. Paul River. What it truly did was, put the country into further economic, political, moral, and financial dependence. What a shame! Big Ben, no remorse; and Uncle Sam, smiled."

Zulu turned to Dr. King.

"Martin," he said, "as the story goes, Liberia had no choice as it's father's son, Borah, in Congress, angrily accused its brother of not paying his debt, or not paying it on time. As a result, their father must allow a gunboat to shell Monrovia until the government look for money to pay back. So, Marcus Garvey of the United Negro Improvement Association, proposed to Uncle Sam's Congress, that he had the mantle to pay all of Liberia's debt, $2,000,000, if Uncle Sam would allow him to transfer his headquarter to Monrovia. His proposal became a political embarrassment for Uncle Sam and Monrovia. In 1924, President King accused Garvey's organization of intensifying racial feelings of hatred and ill will. President King further said that Liberian policy was making of a nation and not of a race."

The gods murmured.

Not waiting for the audience to calm, Zulu Menya asked, "If that is the case, why can't a white man, or children born to white people in Liberia, become a citizen of Liberia? In fact, where is King," he asked, looking around.

"Mr. King has gone into the upper room," someone announced.

"From all indications, Liberia desperately needed that money," Zulu said. "But again, the country was protecting a father who didn't care for him. It is a pity for a love so strong, that a father is not reciprocated."

Zulu Menya's voice dropped, and tears rolled down his cheeks. He was sobbing.

Shocked, the audience grew quiet.

Dr. Tolbert walked to Zulu Menya, tapped his back and said, "It is a pity to struggle for love and affection when it must flow freely. If a child does not get the requisite nurturing from his parents to aid his fullest development, the outcome is difficult to comprehend. You don't have to cry my brother. Just continue the good work."

Zulu Menya wiped his tears, took in his breath and let it out slowly.

Zulu Menya continued, "But over time, King became smart. He knew that all of Liberia's woes came from keeping the country's economic and financial strength in foreign capital. So he decided to reverse it. He saw that it was fruitful. With the revenue the government collected, King opened the interior to create other sources of revenue.

"Keeping the foreign capital in Monrovia, and looking closely at the agent-receiverships, Liberia revenue grew. It was able to pay eight years of the interest on the 1912 loan, as well in 1925. The government generated $25,000,000 within that period. It was the highest revenue collection known of in the history of the country. King now knew that a better financial management system, and keeping eyes on the collectors, could raise the intended revenue. The foreign agents' presence was temporary. But for how long will Liberia keep it that way?" Zulu Menya asked with a chuckle.

"Well, gentlemen, I know you guys are wary of my explanation," Zulu Menya went on, "but in the end, you will know why Mother Supreme had to send the Falcon to the earth, Fricano, especially Liberia. It was transformed along the way before landing in Liberia, and the competing forces opened the nation up to destruction, disgrace, and more dependence of financial, economic, political and moral aids. You will see that Liberia's biggest failure as a nation, has been the ability to appease its creator against all odds. Its greatest self-destructive weapon is the ardent love it has, and the farfetched hopes of its father; allowing him back into his bosom as a legitimate child. Therefore, when Firestone came with its so-called investment, or economic stimulus package, it's long term goal was to rid the land of Briton, French, and the Germans, and changed the British Pound as legal tender. But Ms. Big Ben was finding all possible means to discredit the government, demonstrating in words and deeds as immature and ill prepared to govern its people. All along, there was the pawn system, internal slavery and so many dehumanizing activities. But when the axe was falling on the British plan of a takeover of Liberia, its last hope was the newly established League of Nations, which breathe the Chesty Committee.

"Ladies and gentlemen, let's welcome Tubman and Uncle Sam," Zulu Menya announced.

Tubman got up and started to leave.

"Where are you going, sir?" Zulu Menya asked.

"I am going to the Upper Room," Tubman replied.

"To fast and pray?" Zulu Menya teased.

Tubman did not answer. He kept on walking.

Zulu Menya continued, "All along, Uncle Sam knew that his son had inherited an enormous amount of high quality minerals; Iron ore, bauxite, manganese, mica, zinc, mercury, kyanite, platinum, barite, diamond, gold and the potential for crude oil. So it crept in, taking control of the outcast. When Tubman ascended to the presidency, Uncle Sam pretended (like he always does) that he had a son called, Liberia. Tubman traded in the country to its father during the discovery of iron in Liberia. The list of companies will show that ninety-nine percent of all were wholly, or partly, Uncle Sam's.

"The Liberia Mining Company; established in 1945 by the late iron ore king, Colonel Landsdell Christie. The company was located in Bomi Hills, now called, Bomi Holes, for over nineteen years, exported over 650 million tons of iron ore to feed steel producers in America, Europe, and Asia. It was simple; he could have ordered his son to build factories to only export the finished products. The National Iron Ore Company, formed in 1958, and managed by the Mine Management Associates Limited, shipped its first iron ore in 1961, and in 1968, exported about four million tons of ore. In the end, its exit strategy was to sub contract Padmore's Lofa Construction Company.

"LAMCO joint venture comprises of financial resources of American, Canadian, Liberian and Swedish investors and banks. Bong Mining Company was a company operating on behalf of the Dutch-Liberian Mining Company, DELIMCO. All of these companies poured into Liberia and increased its economy. Its GNP showed signs of greatness, and after their departure, they left giant holes and an impoverished nation. If Uncle Sam meant well for Liberia, it would have made Liberia a part of its industrial base. I now see that Taiwan and others are more valuable and strategic than Liberia."

"How did this happen?" Mohamed Mutala asked.

"All of the financial institutions were wholly, or partly, for Uncle Sam," Zulu Menya replied. "Like the days of the West Africa Bank Limited, where the country revenue generation mechanism and storage were in the hands of others. Liberia, again allowed all of its money and reserved to be decided by Uncle Sam. These are the banks; Bank of Liberia, established 1954 by a public company. It claimed that Liberians were the majority shareholders. Horton will write his side of the story showing the frustration at home and the ascendency to the African Development Bank and Bank of New York. Bank of Monrovia, established October 1, 1935 and an affiliate of the National City Bank, New York. Bank of Monrovia became the official depository of the Republic of Liberia. Chase Manhattan Bank, established 1961, operated and owned by Chase Manhattan Bank of New York.

"The International trust Company was established in 1948;

owned and operated by International bank, Washington, D.C. Liberian Trading and Development Bank, LTD., (TRADEVCO), was established in 1955; owned and operated by Mediobanca Milan, Italy and Bankers Trust Company New York. Commercial Bank of Liberia, established in 1961 and owned by Intra Bank. The Union National Bank (Liberia) INC, established in 1963.

"Let's look at the insurance companies," Zulu Menya continued. "Intrusco Corporation, established 1949 and owned by the International Trust Company of Liberia, Liberian Insurance Agency Incorporated, established in 1964 and owned by Bank of Liberia and W. E. Found & Co. Ltd. London. The La Fondiara Insurance Companies Ltd, was established in 1959 and owned by the Italians and TRADECO. The Royal Exchange Assurance, established in 1962 and owned by the Royal Exchange Assurance of London. And, American International Underwriters, Inc., established in 1963 and owned by the American International Underwriters, Inc.

"Uncle Sam was everywhere in Liberia, like two pieces of sheet glued together; and its elder sons in Liberia, Firestone and the United States Trading Company, legally binding and co-heir, was at the head of the commercial empire fashioned by Uncle Sam to exploit its outcast. There were the West African Explosives and Chemicals, Ltd, Liberian Cement Corporation, the Liberian Industrial Development Corporation, the Liberia Refining Company, the Mesurado Group of Companies, African Fruit Company, Liberia Produce Marketing Corporation, Pan Am, UNIROYAL, and uncountable potential industries.

"Tubman's Liberia was a piece of elephant meat, (as it is said in Liberia) where everyone, con artists, took advantage of the vulnerability of its people and financial status. Its University of Liberia provided quality education (thanks to India) which produced several of Africa academia. The manufacturing sector in Liberia grew at an astronomical height and, its economy was a boom. Uncle Sam still knew that the line separating the country was boiling like a volcano eruption, but it dare not to warm the leadership. That rope was the trigger to unshackle Liberia's illusive economic growth without a foundation. If Uncle Sam truly loved Liberia and wanted to see it flourish, he would have easily done for it what it had to do with the Marshall Plan. Liberia would not have tasted a civil war. Assimilation of different tribal groups would have flowed naturally because of the different companies stationed across the country.

"I have a section called 'Extra' to highlight all major infrastructures from Uncle Sam, which majority of the citizens know it as gifts; John F. Kennedy Memorial Medical Center. The JFK Memorial Medical Center opened in 1970, built out of a $75,000,000 loan from Uncle Sam to Liberia. I wish it had been named, Suacoco Memorial Medical Center," Zulu said sadly.

"The Free Port of Monrovia commenced operation in 1948, and expanded in. It was managed by the Monrovia Port Management Company, Limited, (Headquarters in New York) formed by Delta Steamship Line, Inc. Farrell Lines Inc, Firestone Plantations Company, Mining Company Ltd, Mobil Oil Corporation, Texaco Incorporated and the Liberian Company with the Government of Liberia as one of the stockholders, incorporated in the State of Delaware, U.S.A. Gentlemen, referee and player at the same time... incorporated in the United States, Liberia as a stockholder? Thanks to the establishment of the National Port Authority in 1971.

"For the Mount Coffee hydro power plant, the T.J.R. Faulkner-W.F. Walker Hydroelectric Power Station, a World Bank project,

Liberia received $24,300,000 in 1963. Guess who won the contract for that construction?"

No one responded.

Zulu answered, "Stanley Consultant, Iowa, U.S.A., as Project Managers. Everything about Liberia has an Uncle Sam in it."

Patrick Lumumba voiced, "One may argue that the 1970s recession played a major role in the decline of Liberia."

"It may be true that it may have played a role," Zulu Menya replied. "But a closer look at Liberia's financial pillars, and you wouldn't need a prophet to predate impoverishment. Patrick," Zulu Menya addressed the man, "take a look at Liberia benefits. The country had a hanging economy, an impoverished nation whose citizens' only reflection of the economic boom is the many holes in Mano River, Bomi, Bong Mines and Nimba ranges. Also, an open field which used to host the VOA relayed stations, and another, the remains of the Omega navigation tower; a broken country recovering from the vortex of its folly and sins.

"The greatest lost is the missing middle class; the denial of the full participation of all Liberians into the boom, and not allowing Liberians to be co-heirs to those who had the huge conglomeration of companies. It is unbelievable how Uncle Sam has provided developmental stimulus packages for Taiwan, South Korea, and the manner in which it has brought Haiti and Philippine into its bosom. However, Liberia, its own child, is dashed.

"Therefore, ladies and gentleman, I am proposing to Mother Supreme to send me to Liberia to rid the country of all the strangeness and propose the Back-to-Self Movement, a time to put all childishness away. I will need your support if I am called before the Council of Elders of the Universe to better explain this concept."

"You can count on our support," they all said in unison.

****

As it turned out, Zulu Menya was ordered by Mother Supreme to travel to Liberia, rid it of the strange happenings, and proposed a developmental solution to stimulate self-awareness and growth.

****

Zulu Menya arrived in Liberia with twenty-five million flyers written in various Liberia languages, Liberian English, and English. Through his wiz-omnipresence, he distributed it as a package to everyone, including foreign nationals who were still in the country. Within the package was a flyer with the inscription 'Love thy neighbor as thy self', a white handkerchief to clean oneself, a tin of ashes to spread across the door to scare away the demon which always followed people. It was the major way of contact, and an old Liberian Dollar, which the Central Bank made an acceptable medium of exchange. He visited various community radio stations in the country to discuss his message. Some requested money while others allowed him without charge. Those who allowed him without charge were free within a month, but those who refused it, took time.

On the radio, Zulu Menya said, "My fellow Liberians, I sent you a package and each item has specific meaning and action. If you truly want this curse to leave, share with the person next to you. It is simple… if you have a loaf of bread, cut it into two and give half to your neighbor. Do this until each person has gotten a piece, and within four days time, you will see the difference. If you don't have a neighbor, go out and look for one. And with a smile, share what you have.

"The white handkerchief is to wipe your sweat and wipe your hands when you shake your neighbor's hand. The tin of ashes is for you to spread across the door post and around the house; it will keep the demons from entering. The rusty old coin is, Liberia; if you truly love the country, you will clean it, clear your house and around it, clean your neighborhood, the community, and the nation. If your neighbor cannot do it, help him. Help the old folks and respect them."

Zulu Menya's message was getting, but some political churches took it differently; calling his method demonic. Unscrupulous politicians degraded it as it was meant to fool the people.

"He wants to be president," several persons went on the radio saying.

They used the various civil society as advocacy groups, comprises of the army of unemployed, to go into homes to cease the packages which the politicians ordered to be resold in new parks to the same household. Zulu Menya knew now that the problem was the attitudes of the people, and he single out individuals and institutions with influence and large followings. The most influential institution was the church, followed by other religious institutions. A few businesses benefited from the sales of the so-called solution to the crisis.

Politicians only had strength whenever elections were in sight. Therefore, he contacted the most influential pastors and explained his package in detail. All consignments of fake products were made to expire before entering the country. The pastors took it and spread it around. The citizens accepted and after two months, there were some signs of peace. At last, Liberia was a place of hope and inspirations.

Zulu Menya requested to meet with the three branches of government; he had a proposal for the country. After three months of continual lobbying, he was accepted to address the government at the Capitol Building. Then, he, as an individual, became a subject of discussion all over Liberia. Late one evening, Zulu Menya turned on the radio and this talk show was discussing him.

"Who is Zulu Menya?" One talk show host asked on his Fifty-Twelve program.

"He is a nobody," one caller said. "Why must the government accept a man who had not gone to Harvard or Yale to address the government?"

"I know him, a regular graduate of the Sinkor Assembly of God High," the man continued. "And like us, he went to the University of Liberia. What does he have to offer us?"

"If he was a graduate of St. Patrick, College of West Africa, Ricks Institute, or any other renowned school, he should be honored," a female caller challenged. "But, look at the high school he attended? He had not travelled to Europe or America for education. He has nothing to offer us."

Zulu Menya smiled.

CHAPTER THIRTEEN

In six months time, a patriotic gathering of the three branches of government provided a platform for Zulu Menya to present to the government his action plan for Liberia's growth and development.

"Great leaders of Liberia," Zulu Menya began, "could we sing two songs; The Lone Star Forever and This Land is My Land. As we sing it, let's contemplate on the wordings," he suggested. "The electrifying force of the songs will remind you of Liberia being the only country your birth rights are associated with, and the first country to lead the touch of independence; the flower of Africa. You must jealously protect it, love it, honor and cherish it."

Zulu Menya started the song, The Lone Star Forever.

He looked around the audience as they joined him. In the balcony, among Liberia's academia, he saw people sitting proudly with spectacles at the tips of their noses. He recognized the economists who boasted of greater achievements, but failed miserably to get Liberia out of its present economic status. The politicians, sitting opposite him, well schooled and spoke of impressive designs of improvement, but lacked the mantles to implement a project using the project cycle mechanism. They never saw the need to get the country out of its continuous impoverishment. They always saw a rich Liberia because of its natural resources which they, without remorse, exploited; deliberately refusing to create rich Liberians by creating jobs for everyone to live in the resource rich Liberia.

Their strategies are to keep the people in abject poverty. Zulu Menya knew they were packs of wolves, viciously at each other throats, the real enemies of the country; making sure to destroy in broad daylight, anyone who opposed the modus operandi of their organization. Their organization, the Babylon Harlot Cup, an insatiable bottomless cup, which seeks to unite their body, mind, and spirit with the sole intent to cherish self rather than country. The wine of nepotism and sycophancy, used as a daily tonic, made them intolerance that they would use the necromancy to destroy their foes. Zulu Menya was aware of the disgusting wolves, mainly politicians, who had taken over the House of the People; appearing in angelic garments, but had always opted to further divide Liberia into tiny pieces in the name of representation. The overall betterment of Liberia was far below those tiny constituencies. Rather, they were fighting greatly to maintain power by sucking to drain all the goodies out of Liberia. All their projects were based on the strategies of mass production, making their constituents to always want more while looking up to them as liberators.

Zulu Menya noticed a few men dressed in black robes, sitting close to the so-called politicians. He knew they were the wise men who bragged of their supremacy over Solomon's wisdom of deciding cases. They were wise enough to know that laws were not to be interpreted to satisfy personal interests, but for the general good of the country and its citizenry. He saw the Ph.Ds, whose presence in the country made Liberia and students to struggle for textbooks. The sixth generation of the civilized people, sitting next to their opponents. He knew they missed their power; especially if it is a one man show and for the resources. It was no more a family matter. All they did now was collecting royalties from infrastructures their forefathers built with funds from the country's coffers.

The remnants of the 'Rice Riot' who still had grips on political power, were also seated. They were all staring directly at him. Zulu Menya smiled at them. He was aware they only knew how to destroy, but had never proposed a tangible solution to the backwardness Liberia found itself in. Their intoxicating portion of criticisms without solutions, vandalism, intolerance, badmouthing the country and individuals with honest motives, sycophancy, nepotism, corruption and prowling the country's resources which they borrow from the 'civilized people'. It had all spread like wildfire throughout the country. Importantly, their virus had taken over the young minds, whose only solution to a situation is destruction of lives and properties.

The audience completed the two songs.

Zulu Menya noticed all eyes focused on him. Fears overcame him. He took in a deep breath, unfolded the piece of paper before him, and placed it on the podium.

"I am a Liberian," he started, "and that makes me special. It doesn't matter what school I went to. What matter is, Liberia, the country I love so dearly. Like the last song says,

'This land is my land, this land is your land; from
Monteserrado to the Nimba Mountain...,'

"This plan I have in my hand is called, Action Liberia," Zulu Menya continued. "It is divided into several strategic segments and sub segments."

The hall was quiet at first. Then there was murmuring, and later, a loud shout, like those of battle cries. It had started outside.

The Sergeant at Arm whispered something to the Speaker, and then to the three other officers with him. One approached the President, one went to the Chief Justice, and the last officer approached the Senate Pro Tempore.

People were outside demonstrating against the sealed proposal. Zulu Menya knew it was the most upgraded, commonly used crazy call-to-action, in present day Liberia by young people who believes in empty talks. A few dollars could silence their action, but he had no money. He looked toward the Speaker, who signaled him to commence his discussion.

Zulu Menya did.

"What kind of Liberia do you want," he asked the audience. When nobody answered, Zulu Menya asked, "Don't you have a picture, in mind, of the kind of country you all want? The Liberia I see has no clear-cut direction; no plans to take the people from one level to another, no plans to unite and reconcile the country. Can't you see the conditions of the country in which you live? It is divided; the rich and powerful against the poor. The next generation is not mentored, nor nurture; children are all on the streets, majority of our young girls are selling their body for survival, schools are incompetents, hospitals have become killing fields, unemployment is high, hope is dashed, people are angry and frustrated, lies and witch-hunting have engulfed the country, low level of self-esteem, saving is low, the future is bleak, self love and dishonesty are sucking the country out of its juice, dirt have enveloped the country, no care and respect for the country, our elderly, nor the dead. There is no culture to hold onto, and the economy is above the people.

"What are you doing to this country and for the people? Sending your children abroad will not help, they will have to come back to their fatherland and meet the same people. If the people aren't taken care of, and develop fully, your children will not live in peace.

"How many of you know what it's like to go to sleep without eating? How about being unemployed? Their children are out of school, or have nowhere to sleep. These are their daily conditions, and they have instructed you with the power to get them get out of poverty.

"All aspect of Liberia, and its people, need long term repairs," Zulu Menya continued. "I'm not a political scientist, an economist, or a savior who has all the solutions to our country. But I'm a humbled and practical man who has an ardent love for Liberia. My love surpassed all of you, had it not been so, you would have acted.

"I do believe, transforming Liberia into a prosperous country requires the valor and determination of the few earlier settlers. They were not perfect, but struggled to survive and proved to their creator, the status code; that indeed they can make it. I am not like some of those people who killed and destroyed and are now proposing solutions. We all know that most of those who killed indiscriminately suffered terribly. Some became crazy and died, while the few who are alive are like the living dead, struggling with continual nightmare. Mother Supreme gave them a grace period to repent, or be punished by the international enforcer of the laws. Uncle Sam saw them kill and destroy, but did nothing. And, may not do anything; his usual pretense.

"As I said earlier, few of the settlers knew the value of this country. They knew what it was like to be called a freed man, and be proud of it. So they came and saw, calling their findings Liberia, and demonstrating their desire for freedom and self-governance. They wrote an anthem to show and tell the world their passion for freedom, which took them to the land of their forefathers. At the same time, they were choked by global forces, and all they had available was their inner strength and trust in God above.

"Your ancestors, because they love you and wanted you to stay on course, reaffirmed their passion for this land through Edwin Barclay's poem, 'The Lone Star for Ever'. I recommend that every Liberian, abroad and at home, or at school… at work, wherever you are, every morning when you wake up, sing the chorus of the 'Lone Star forever'. A lot of good plans have been put into place, but my recommendations are supplementary to the structures or plans the government has put in place. Honorable and good people of Liberia, accept my suggestion for us to sing the last chorus of Liberia's only patriotic song, 'The Lone Star Forever'."

Zulu Menya began singing,

> "'The Lone Star forever! The Lone Star forever! O long may it float over land and over sea. Desert it, no never! Uphold it, forever! O shout for the Lone Star banner, All hail,'"

He ended with a smile.

"It's a great song," Zulu Menya said. "My people, the first major problem is, identity. This is the result of a long term adoption, apprenticeship, and wardship practiced by some settlers. It grew worse when names were changed from native to American names, especially with the introduction of the entire country to western clothing and lifestyles. I will openly say, Uncle Sam is the master craftsman in destroying identities and culture of the inhabitants; including the settlers and the prime implements. It was a psychological overhaul of the people, their culture, and their existence. Since then, Liberians have never felt loyal to their country, but rather to the United States. Yet, nobody has openly blamed the United States for most of Liberia's woes. If I may ask, Who is a Liberian?"

No one answered.

Zulu Menya said, "I can still recall the names, Zulu, Badu, Kamara, Ilos, Okai, Kofi, Togar, Sackor, Blay, Dan, Johnson, McGee, Paygar, Bility, Konneh, Captan, and Modad. These are names that show people with different backgrounds; your diversity is your strength. Cherish it to the fullest. It places you above the rest of Africa. And note that we all came here for one particular reason, FREEDOM. This is why our country is called, Liberia. We are here to provide the space and means for those who are being prosecuted, rejected, abandoned, frustrated, and those searching for hope and aspiration, and a place to call home. We love strangers; we provide for them and secure them. Those values make us who we are, Liberians. Instead of holding on to those things that united us, we are further (like the days of old, before the suffering) preaching and holding onto things that are slowly dividing us again. Are we so blind that we cannot see the writing on the wall?"

The hall was quiet.

Zulu Menya had their undivided attention.

"Listen to the words of St. Paul," he emphatically urged.

> 'For, brethren, we have been called to liberty; use not liberty to the occasion of the flesh, but by love serves one another. For all the law is fulfilled in one word, even in this; thou shall love thy neighbor as thy self. When I was a child, I spoke as a child, I understood as a child, I thought as a child; but when I became a man, I put away all childish things.'

"The first childish thing is to leave the Congo-Natives arguments," Zulu Menya said. "You may write about it, and let it be part of our history. The second childish thing is religion, let it be that all men worship God to his liking, and let the dominance be seen in an abstract manner. Take religion from the state or politics. Politicians will always use it for selfish gains. The third childish thing is, stop cursing your country. Love it, and strive to make it a better place."

At this time, Zulu Menya took a sip of his glass of water.

"The fourth childish thing is, stop keeping your citizen away in the name of dual citizenship," he said, setting the glass of water down. "Allow your children to feel free to come home with dignity and respect, no matter what they did, or what other citizenship they took upon. The fifth childish thing is, make Liberia the big brother of Africa, becoming an example to emulate. The sixth childish thing is, stop closing your eyes to the suffering and division, stuffing your ears with tons of cotton so you cannot hear their cry.

"God!" Zulu Menya broke down.

Everyone stared.

He pulled a handkerchief from his pocket and wiped his tears.

"What is wrong with everyone?" he asked. "Can't you see? What have blinded you? Why have you turned your face away from;

"The fact that your future generations are cut off from all those antidotes to making them achieve their full potential. Look at all those children on the streets! Look at the amount of teenagers entering into prostitution, or getting married early! Look at your city, see how dirty it is! Look at how this country is stratified, rich and poor! Semi urban and rural interiors, semi-schooled and self grown. How soon have you forgotten, these evils were the same thing that led the country to self-destruction. National wealth, not equally distributed, corruption and nepotism, the haves and have-nots, the schooled and unschooled, the number of those unemployed, the disregard for public properties, and dependency.

"The fact that your educational system has taken a dangerous downward trend. By sending your children abroad to learn will not solve the problem. Everyone needs to tighten his belt in paying

attention to this only means of getting a fully developed generation of Liberians.

"That your hospitals and health centers are not being monitored and evaluated. Don't you have time for the well being of your citizenry? Who certifies an individual to operate a center? What proves that he is capable of handling health issues? Can't you see my people? Where is the love for the people and the country? This country is the only country for you, and the people are your people! Open your eyes; too many people are suffering and too many are sad. And, only a few people have everything! In a resource rich country, the bulk of the people are poor. It is totally unacceptable, and a shame. This could trigger another civil war!

"That arts and culture are vanishing;

"That the people are looking to other countries for language, behavior, morality, standards, etc.

"The greatest weakness our country is faced with is the dependency syndrome," he continued. "This is the time that all Liberians rid their mind that the United States is their founding father, and that they must depend on it for all necessary life supports. Put Uncle Sam aside, and mention him in your history books! He doesn't teach his offsprings about you. Don't please him, but do business with him like the others, according to the rules. Depend on yourself, your will, your life, and utilize all God-given resources available at your deposal with sincerity and love. Work harder, like you want to prove things!

"Liberia is an outcast of the United State. Over a hundred years, the hope of appeasing the United States has endangered the country and its people. It is time to stand like a man and tell your father, who lied. An NGO colonized you. What you stand for, and believed in; leaving injustices in the United States and founding a country in Africa to call your own, freed from the vices within Uncle Sam's grips. Show your children the good side of Liberia. Tell them about great heroes; even if they are not real, create several to feed their young minds. Reward any child for bravery, intelligence, quality creative and artistic works, and inventions. Tell them about folktales heroes like spiders, and use these folktales to teach morals. Pride yourself with dignity, parade in splendor, rid your mind of him and forgive him.

"Liberia is the apple of God's eye. Can't you see how blessed this country is? Can't you see how blessed you are? Like a beautiful girl among several women, protect yourself from exploitation. Keep your head up, coat your body with clay and after your bath, spread olive oil all over your lovely body. Smile as you moved along the path of life. Do you want a man who will treat you like trash? Stop depending on Uncle Sam; he doesn't care about you. He treats you like a so-called partner, but accepts him like a partner based on the terms and conditions. Love your citizens. Protect them. Make other nations envious of them. Develop everyone as a quality asset. Liberians are special, market your people. Sell what Michael Jackson saw in your women, and sang a lovely song.

"Liberians, it is time you leave used things; clothes, cars, etc. Strived to buy or invent all things new. Elevate yourself from a begging nation, to a progressive one. This country is blessed with great things.

"Calypso Rose sang about your food, pepper soup. Don't you know that your food revolutionized West Africa during the civil war? Market it for returns. Again, Michael Jackson sang about your girls. Protect them and make them proud; make them second to none. Liberians must market these God-given qualities. They will distinguish you from the rest of Africa. We made the best quilts, re-invest in it. After all, Bong and Lofa Counties are noted for making the best kentil cloth; invest in it.

"Several suitors will come by proposing, but being careful in your selection of the right suitor will make your father value you. I know it will take some time, but a journey now will surely take you to your heart's desire. This is why Liberia must focus on making its entire development plan a medium, or long term. Look for partners who will connect your cities with quality road network, encourage Liberians to invest in different means of transportations, various infrastructures, and commercial agricultural initiatives. Learn from Brazil, how to get your people out of the slum. Look at Tanzania and Rwanda for leadership, development, and cleanliness. Look at Singapore for clean water and sanitation. Develop close tie with South Korea, and learned from their success in science, technology, commerce and marketable skills.

"A holistic and inclusive plan so that everyone, despite your orientation, will involve developing Liberian's golden arch in every county. Develop and promote Liberians whose businesses are moving upward. Give them the support, and if possible, funding and tax holidays.

"Secondly, legalize the Liberian English, or Bassa, as a second national language, taught in schools; along with the international English. And, Bassa, being the primary national dialect for convenience or secrecy. I observed that Bassa is easily adaptable, musical, and easily understood. Make it mandatory, and defiance by any person, or institution, should be punishable by law. Don't pretend that you don't know that Liberians are considered as people who don't speak English. International schools, most often, request for test for English Language efficiency.

"Liberian English must be used in songs, written in poems and recited in schools and street corners. It must be discussed in the street corners, the marketplace, the radio, converse with it with love and happiness; make others to love it when in Liberia or abroad. Take notes of it pronunciation and create dictionaries to define and incorporate new works. It is time to promote and protect Liberia's creativity by enforcing the copyright laws. Lawbreakers must be seriously punished.

"Thirdly, Liberia needs to invest in a national database and a backup system. The government must embark on a vigorous campaign to add every soul within the country; including those being born during the campaign. This system will provide citizens and foreign nationals with identification numbers and cards. The ID card will contain all information pertaining to an individual, and will enable him to access education, health care centers, etc. Each town, or combined town, within each region must have four mobile fingerprinting facilities assigned at clinics to feed into the district database headquarter and shared with the regional and national database system. An individual can access his information from any part of the country. Accessing hospitals, clinics, healthcare centers, schools, etc, can be done through the identification number and made mandatory. This system, if established, will boost national security and strengthen the house of statistics. It is a very expensive venture, but the government must make this a priority, and the outcome will be rewarding.

"One of the greatest problems Liberia is faced with now is the land crisis. Observer says these places the country into a fragile situation of civil conflict. The government must re-survey all demarcation of counties and districts, down to the chiefdoms; and maintain regional boundaries as official. During this process, it must be mandated that everyone, including administrators, bring along their copies of the title deeds for verification. Although it is a costly venture, but it will surely lay the foundation for a legislation that will empower the government to take control of this asset. Although traditional lands will be owned ceremoniously by those in control, but all land belongs to the government. Government must be aware of the sales, and buyers must provide a comprehensive plan of its development. All private individuals who have over a hundred acres, and have not developed it, the government must be authorized to co-owned the land, find possible investment and rent it where the owners and the government will profit from the returns. It must be a criminal act, non-billable, with a penalty of forty-five to fifty years in prison for anyone who will sell, or resell land, or sell land to two or more persons. All undeveloped land within city limit must be given to the government, who will find a renter to build a certified structure. The owners must receive their just reward.

"The government must use its arable land for its economic recovery programs with special emphasis on the growth corridors. To restore the export base of the country, the government must rehabilitate the cocoa, timber, coffee, fishery, infrastructure, and transport. Each county operating its own, what used to be 'Money Bus' System, find new modes, or create an enabling environment for people to move from one place to another, water supply, and communication sectors. The national government must encourage and invest, with a Liberian at the head of all levels, shareholders in agricultural projects. Every investment must be mandated to have a downstream approach, where Liberians will be empowered to take charge and employ other Liberians.

"For example: If electricity is supplied by LEC to Monrovia, the city must be divided into regions and Liberian entrepreneurs will be sub-contracted to employ others to complete the distribution of electricity within that particular region. Those entrepreneurs will, at the end of the period, give LEC its appropriate allotments. Special relation must be established with Ivory Coast, Ghana, Nigeria, and Guinea, where Liberian farmers will internalize and improve upon success stories from farmers of those countries.

"Apply all technologies that will lead the country to reaching self-sufficiency, if possible, in a week's time, and invest in the domestication of animals and fowls to save the endanger species. The conservation laws must be revisited and violators must be charged and jailed for seventy years without bail. Liberia must ask Rwanda about its cleanliness policy, adopted it and internalized it to its situation.

"The forestry development authority must live up to its name by replanting trees as logging companies have almost finished depleting the forest. The reserved forest must be jealously protected, and any institution, or individual, caught must face the full weight of the laws. A hundred-year sentence without bail must be the penalty for violators.

"Gentlemen, in collaboration with the Ministry of Public

Works and Education, and the proposed Ministry of Water, all companies, logging, mining, all others, must construct concrete bridges. They must be designed and attested by the engineering association and approved by ministry of works throughout their concessional areas. All housing units, reflecting all basic services, must be of a standard approved by the Ministry of Works.

"Liberia is blessed with an abundance of water, making it easier to get water from a creek or river and stored in large reservoirs and purified; allowing it to flow to each household. The government must discourage the digging of hand pumps and building of outdoor latrines by individuals and institutions. The statutory agency must continually check the operational plans, and all projects of nongovernmental organizations; making sure their interventions are in line with government development agendas. Any institution refusing to cooperate, or honor this law, must be prosecuted and deported.

"The educational system is considered a mess; this has been the slogan. But what method is available to get it out of its messy state? What are you doing to restore its values? Is the ten-year master plan the antidotes to take the country out of this educational slum? I believe restoring the values required the full cooperation of all parents, teachers, communities, religious institutions, government and partners; just about everyone.

"The first step is to rid dishonesty from schools, especially for teachers; they should spend twenty-five years in jail with no billable term, and their teaching license revoked. And for students caught, should be jailed for three years with a year of community service. A rating and award system, for both private and government schools, is to be conducted by civil society organizations. They should partner with the government and use the outcomes to probe institutions. All schools must be rated by independent bodies, and the government takes seriously the outcomes. Specialized or special courses must be part of all high school curriculum. For example, if a pupil has excellent grades in biology and chemistry, he must be scouted to take specialized courses along with high school subjects in preparation for entry into the medical school. After four years, that pupil must be able to go further into specialized areas of medicines. Therefore, if we want more medical practitioners and doctors, let's look back at all age-old curriculums."

"All pupils must be mandated to take a master of achievement tests at the end of every school year. This test must be administered by a special educational task force comprising of civil society organizations, and the national results be published or posted. This must be a requirement for promotion to the next class. It must be mandatory and carried a non-billable criminal penalty, follow by one-year community service, if a school, or teacher, promotes students who failed the test. Teacher-student relationship with an immoral undertone, sexual contact, corruption, etc, must be a criminal offense, and liable to life in prison.

"The Education Ministry, in collaboration with the Ministry of Health and Agriculture, must introduce the care-food program where a free lunch, made from selected nutritional crops grown in Liberia, is given to pupils for breakfast and lunch. Each district must select its own farmers within its region to supply those crops. A free lunch program made with local crops, may help reduce malnutrition across the country. From pre-school to high school, tolerance must be taught and also be a yardstick for promotion.

"The national county meet must be turned into an annual or biannual league. All counties must use all available resources to support the county team named after that county. The counties must establish a competitive league where all the best players will form the county team. This team will contest in the national league.

"It is time for the Ministry of Health to promote the use of traditional herbs. Local herbalists must be allowed, and given the capitals, to operate their own clinic or healing centers. The ministry must constantly monitor and carried out a continual evaluation to enable the facilities to meet the expected standard. A long-term plan to create research facilities must begin with the medical schools. Liberians must stop demonizing these gifted people as witches and wizards. Their medication must be sold on the market with the prescribe doses written.

"The social welfare component be removed from the ministry and be merged with the national social security, and the group of seventy-seven. Its program must mainly cover and cater to the elderly, those with disability and the unemployed. It must aim at creating hope for after employment, but not to build luxurious complex. The function belongs to the housing authority. It must form a partnership with the housing authority to build care centers where the elderly will be catering for. Certified Liberians owned organizations must operate these care centers. The Ministry of Health must conduct a constant monitoring system and the centers receive ratings from civil society organizations. The social welfare must have a long term plan, to respect the elderly and not make them come to the cities to get their little benefits. It must develop a holistic program for children in the streets. It must have the authority to hold parents responsible for certain levels of abandonment. Every infrastructure, or technology, must be built to accommodate those with disabilities.

"All community colleges must be transformed into technical

or vocational schools with a two-year learning period. One year for training, and the last year for implementation. Success at the level of implementations will qualify the student for graduation. Ingenious or inventive students, or students with specialties at all levels, must be selected based on merit and sent to universities at home, or abroad for further trainings. Upon completion, they must be given seed capital for entrepreneurial development, or placed in strategic positions, well paid to protect Liberia's interests.

"The Medical School must be separated from the University of Liberia, and elevated to a teaching and research university with two other facilities open between Bong and Lofa, and River Gee and Grand Gedeh Counties. It must operate a four-year program, and another two years of specialization. Most of its prerequisite courses must be sent to high schools, and students who wants to enter the medical school take those courses alongside their regular high school subjects. The medical school must incubate the Liberia's Institute of Biological Research.

"The Tubman National Institutes for Medical Agency must be independent and allowed to operate a four-year degree granting program. Two other facilitators of the TNIMAs must be open between Bomi and Gbarpulu Counties, and other between Rivercess and Sinoe Counties. The Law School must be a four-year degree granting program. All public universities must add a research component to their operations and, moved into more specialized areas other than the usual courses. The colleges of Agriculture and Forestry must be relocated to CARI. The Maritime Institute must be elevated to a full degree granting program. The College of Science and Technology must be situated outside of the Firestone Plantation Company, across the Farmington River around division thirty-one. The government must make all public high school run partly vocational. All teacher programs must be elevated to an AA degree granting programs, with possibility of graduates to enter into the College of Education. A special relation must be reestablished with Tuskegee for BWI to be elevated to a technical college, and placed under the commission for higher education. Berea College in the USA or other colleges and universities in the USA, and other countries formed special bonds through the intervention of the Commission of Higher Education to create special bonds with universities and colleges in Liberia.

"Liberia must begin to accept dual citizenship, and place special emphasis on finding over three thousand Liberian scientists, engineers, and medical or other experts in the Diasporas. Special privileges must be given to these heroes. Liberia must also tap into the academic strength of other countries, especially India, Nigeria, and Cuba, by inviting professors, current or retired, with certain qualities acceptable to the country institutional development. Revisit the constitution, or make use of where it accepts people of Negro descent, by inviting black poets, artists, inventors, professional, investors, from around the world and provide them with the enabling environment to feel at home. This arrangement must be the sole responsibility of the national government and monitored by the local or regional government. Children born in Liberia must be granted citizenship despite the colors of their skin, and receive birth certificate right upon delivery. The constitutional clause with racial undertone be revisited, and other people who aren't black receive conditional citizenship. The clause be written as part of our history.

"Over the years, there have been massive influxes into Monrovia from the rural areas. This movement has affected agriculture, already destroyed by the cash crop, rubber, and saw an urban explosion. All water and sanitation activities within the urban communities, especially Monrovia, already destroyed by the civil war, are overwhelmed. The drainages or sewer systems and motor roads suffered when it rained. A Ministry of Water, Environment and Sewer (combining all WASH activities from public works, health, land and mines, water and sewer, city government and environmental agency) established to focus directly on how to plan and implement an overhaul of the water, waste, sewer systems at the at urban and local areas. Water and Sewer must be totally dissolved because it is a service provider. That ministry must clear all houses along the Mesurado River and create a distance between residential and business houses from the ocean, and the bodies of water; mainly the Du River.

"Future motor roads along the river may transform the face of the water and the city. It may generate additional resources from boat rides, and other water sports. A criminal penalty of one hundred thousand Liberian Dollars, or life imprisonment, will protect the water from contamination and environmental pollution. It will also ease the traffic in Sinkor and Jallah Town. A tunnel, with toll, under the ramp at the James Spring Field to Airfield short cut, will ease the traffic at the Vamoma Junction.

"Enforcing the zoning laws, with some amendments, will create an organized country which will enhance the postal system, ease the fighting of crime. The National government ensures that all communities in Monrovia be divided by motor roads, and at least all counties are connected by a transport system; rail, paved roads, water supply, and basic life improvement facilities. It seems difficult and expensive, but managing our meager resources and venturing into possible revenue generating options other than the traditional ones, we can surely do it."

The audience murmured.

Someone asked, "How will the government pay for all those activities?"

"Connect all of your county capitals with paved roads. This will show development, and taxes collected properly, will increase the coffers. Focus on a six-year national manpower development strategies; your citizens are the major possessions. Look to the several nontraditional sources of generating resources. Besides, states are like people, make friends and manage wisely."

CHAPTER FOURTEEN

"I am proposing to divide Liberia into three regions; western, central and eastern," Zulu Menya continued, after their hour long break. "This is not in line with the constitution, but I believe this stratification will aid the central government in its control process. Each region must be further demarcated into sub-division for administrative purposes. This will rid the country of its language and tribal attachments, which has a disjointed political, social, and cultural undertone that can easily plunge the country into another civil conflict.

"It is good for the redistribution of wealth and labor, and equal political and economic participation. Each region must be void of Monrovia political interference, and identify with political and economic capitals. The political capital must host regional administration and head of region, paved the way for monitoring and evaluating of those at the bottom of the political ladder. Let all regional authorities, except the town chiefs, be elected by the people. A single ballot paper will allow voters to select the president, vice president, senators and legislators, superintendent, district leaderships, and heads of auditing commission and anti-corruption agency.

"Besides, each region must be represented at the national level by eighteen senators and twenty-four legislators (elected by popular votes) who is representing all the sub-divisions. Each region must have the power to negotiate concessions, collect and impose taxes, make laws, run their own police unit, and contribute to the national coffers. The region must be accountable to them and shared monthly reports with the central government. Regional projects must be identified for regional development, and regional policies for growth must be proposed annually.

"The central government must conduct periodic audits through the auditing commission or collaborating with an independent firm on all projects. The economic capital must be solely for construction of factories and must host all large firms. Firms with the potential for vast employment and growth must be spread across the regions. Goods from those firms must be distributed to consumers in any part of the country. The national government will have the power to decide cases referred from each region responsible for national security, including heads of police commissioners, deciding fiscal and monetary policies. They must develop a national standard of development for regions to follow, receive all reports from the leaderships of regions, and monitor all developmental projects. In order to maintain checks and balance between the implementing of the arms of governance, it must be enacted that partition from the people can only remove the heads of all institutions of accountability.

"The auditing commission and transparency commission are to be responsible to prepare a quarterly report on individual activities and present a twenty-one member, randomly selected distinguished elders, from across the country. They would be appointed by the president to monitor and evaluate the report. Those elders must only serve two terms, and are to be exempted from persecutions before or after performing their duties.

"The Executive Branch needs to be completely repaired, knowing that development means cooperation and collaboration from all parties involved in a piece of work. Every law must be enforced, monitored, and culprits persecuted by the appropriate agencies. The biggest weaknesses in Liberia are to follow-up on action points, or constantly enforced a law, or the lack of the will power to carry out post project evaluation.

"When you are the person responsible to punish someone who breaks a law in accordance with the law, it is patriotism. Liberia will not progress unless lawbreakers, no matter what their status is, are dealt with in line with the laws. We need, what Liberians call in the Liberia English, dry-face, to move this country forward. The president needs a panel of experts who will do due diligence of all appointees."

Zulu Menya paused, and wiped sweat off his face.

"Before taking office," he continued, "all senior appointees must present a realistic six-month plan with achievable goals on how he will manage and operate the office. A unit within the presidency, and the General Auditing Commission, must be responsible to appraise the person after his initial six months. A post, evaluation findings, must be presented to the president, and made public. The recommendations within the findings must qualify the person for another six months or be persecuted according to the laws. Then, he must again provide another six-month plan of action. This must be the fate of all appointees.

"The president must maintain an Economic Management Team, or create an Economic Advisory Council, which must include the Minister of Finance, the Central Bank, Agricultures, Commerce, Labor, Public Works, the Ministry of Water, and the House of Statistic, the university, and the National Investment Commission, as statutory members. Other ministries and agencies will be called upon when needed. The council must provide economic analysis and advice the president on a wide range of domestic and international policy issues. It must aim at achieving full employment, full production, and stable prices, look at the consumers' side of the production, review all concessions, and evaluate the use of the Liberian Dollar, or United States Dollar, as the only medium of exchange. To make it mandatory, and punishable by law without bail, if anyone refuses the Liberian Dollar, no matter the conditions; implementing, or monitoring arms must be a program unit. Discussion must be short and targeted at reaching a desired goal. It must void its self of all bureaucracies, but maintain a goal getting direction.

"All senior and junior advisors to the President must be mandated to present, on a quarterly basis, a complete work plan through the office of the Chief of Staff to the President. He must match activities against implementation. All departments and ministries within the Ministry of States, must on a monthly basis, report its activities; including those on processes, procedures, and activities to the office of the Deputy Minister of Administration who will then prepare a quarterly report and present it to the Chief of Staff and further discuss with the President.

"The central bank and Ministry of Finance must, in collaboration with the Ministry of Commerce, especially the small medium enterprise unit, and the Liberian Business Association, scouts financing options for all SMEs. The fund must be managed by the unit and be open to audit in collaboration with a designated Liberian bank loan, money to develop the sectors.

"A three-month tax holiday must be given to all new Liberian businesses. A monthly training, or weekly monitoring, will enable SMEs to grow. The Central Bank must discourage and recommend prosecution of all financial institutions, whose sole intend is to exploit the Liberian people by giving loans and requesting high interest rates. The economic council must, on a quarterly basis, assess all loan portfolios. With the database system, debtors should be persecuted through a fast track court. The Central Bank must revisit the insurance policy and make sure the package benefits the Liberian people. Everyone, also businesses, must be encouraged to take advantage of insurance opportunity.

"The Government must make sure that the insurance agencies are credible. The credit court must be extended to all counties, and debtors severely dealt with according to the reformed laws. The Ministry of Finance must pay all domestic debts, and begin by giving tax returns to Liberian Businessmen and entrepreneurs.

"State owned enterprises are all powerful because the government has not developed the will power to look at their benefits, managerial effectiveness, and ownership. Who monitors states owned enterprises? Who do they report to, and to whom are they accountable?" Zulu Menya asked.

When no one answered, he asked, "Can state owned enterprises be independent, or partly independent?"

No one answered.

Zulu Menya barked, "The investment commission must learn from the mistakes of the so-called Liberia economic boom of the 1960s! Do you know that no Liberian was part of all of the companies who looted Liberia? Others will argue that Padmore benefited, but the National Iron Company knew that it had sucked all the ore, and used Padmore as an exit strategy.

"I will suggest that the commission, in collaboration with the economic council team, creates within all concessions a local contents where government sponsored Liberians will have, if not more, at least fifty percent. Any Liberian who will be caught fronting for foreign nationals without equal partnership, and greater control, must be punished according to the law. The person, or persons, must be given a non-billable sentence. The Bureau of Concession must make sure that all provisions, within the concession agreements related to the number of Liberians to hire and train, be implemented to the fullest.

"In line with the Ministry of Labor and the various universities, the Bureau of Concession must have a complete shared database of all students who are beneficiary of scholarship, proposed by each company in its concessional agreements. A voluntary team comprises of all stakeholders will vet applicants, including international training opportunities, and those opting for science and technology, be prioritized. The commissioner of higher education, and the Ministry of Education, in collaboration with the civil service agency, and representative of the office of the president, must vet all local scholarships with specific focus on specialization in areas that are actually needed in Liberia. With the hydro soon to come on, a special financial package, or extra privilege, must be set aside by the government for manufacturing companies.

"All political capitals must organize an annual creative fairs to promote inventions. Economic capitals proposed, must find time for agricultural fairs to spur growth and self-sufficiency. Liberians must be rewarded for everything during the fairs. A simple example is, Saniquelle and Ganta. Liberians must think out of the box to create anything that will resurrect the Liberian people from the poverty line, and into the mainstream of great powers in West Africa. The religious community, the traditional council, and parents must work with all to taking Liberia to that level.

"The oil company must be discouraged from sending, to be trained, only managers in the oil sector. It must either use the money gathered for training to equip, with state of the art technology, all technical colleges to train those who will do the actual oil work; like welding, plumbing, et cetera. The Bureau of Concession, in monitoring, must make sure the companies are working in line with their proposal.

"The Labor ministry, and other entities, must look thoroughly at the capacity development plans. Labor and the civil service must redirect their attention to the movement of low income workers into better paying positions in various cities and towns. Have a decent pay scale for all government employees; executive, judiciary, and legislative branches of government. Labor must wrestle with the legislators to pass into laws a national standard of minimum wage, considering the everyday increase in the cost of living.

"The housing authority must be revised to push for the rights for all Liberians to own descent homes, and harassed the House to pass into law a national standard cost for a house rental; looking closely at geographical locations. A comprehensive real estate plan to spur growth must be developed by the housing authority. This plan must focus on creating Liberian tycoons.

"The clause forbidding white ownership of land, is historical; it was the source of founding Liberia, but must be made flexible in some cases. Any white individual who has spent over thirty years consistently living in the country, and have huge investment worth over five million dollars, must be considered. He must not hold top level governmental positions. White children, or children of other nationalities born in the country must automatically become citizens. The constitution has given them that rights.

"The Foreign Ministry must review quarterly all protocols or communiqués with other nations. Those with educational cooperation, security and economic cooperation, are sent to the appropriate entities for a speedy response. The unit within the presidency must conduct a post evaluation of the implementations.

"Tourism must go independent, as well as culture. Culture must develop a strategy to boost the sector. A master plan to conserve, develop, and maintain all historical sites, must be established. A national, or several trusts with particular emphasis, must be organized by private citizens to manage those historical sites according to the mandate and guidelines of the governing agency. The General Auditing Commission must leave the old mansion. The building must be transformed into a historical attraction with a room for, if possible, all presidents. All photos and artifacts must be used to tell a story of those presidents. This will provide income to pay staff and maintain the site. A bodies of water, musical reforms, artistic development, costumes, and a national day, must be dedicated to celebrating different aspects of our lives."

Zulu Menya showed, through a blueprint, that traditional sources of income for government need compliments, and tourism is the ideal antidote. He proposed that the beaches be cleaned, and anyone caught dishonoring it, face serious penalties; maybe a fine of one hundred thousand Liberian Dollars, or twenty-five years imprisonment. Beaches in Rivercess, and along the coast, must be given out to a Liberian-foreign collaboration, and well developed to the extent that any visitor, sipping Liberian cherry wine, will always remember the worth of his money.

"It is possible to make Liberia the Caribbean in Africa," Zulu Menya declared. "It is innovation and dedication that can take Liberia to that level.

"Legislators, find your missing link!" he shouted. "Identify yourself and stop hiding behind the honorable statuses. The public needs to prosecute you if you are immoral, while in office, and prosecute you even if you are out of office. All appointed, or elected, officials of government, by law, must declare his assets, and a compulsory post audit be carried out by the audit commission. If the person is free and has served well, the commission and accountability commission will certify him and he must take the results to the designated court where the individual will receive a notarized clearance.

"Members of the Supreme Court must be audited when leaving office. Judges must be punished by law if they are corrupt, or break the law. The Bar Association must also bar any judge, or lawyer, who contravened the profession. The court must be rid of a mason, or poro society. It must be punishable by the law; barring for life or sentencing for twenty five years, if any judge or lawyer used any secret cults to alter justice. Jurors who take bribes, or get caught, be tried; and if guilty, spend a lifetime in jail. Witnesses who lied under oath, must be punished by the laws and spend twenty-five years in prison. Judges and lawyers, or jurors, must be trained periodically, and constantly reminded about the laws governing their professions.

"The Justice Ministry must seek to punish, send to fifteen years any officers without bail; police, immigration, et cetera, who receive bribes while on duty. As the country being exposed to other nationals, it is time that Liberia revisits its criminal laws, and all international protocols relative to maintaining laws and orders. A rapid response force to curb armed robbery, must be fully functional. A tooth-for-tooth law is necessary for all armed robbers, and all collaborators.

"The media must shift from the platform for ads and political news to an instrument for development, spreading the good news of identity, promoting Liberian cultures and arts, sourcing and promoting music and individuals, and exposing and aiding government in the fight against corruption. Fully bringing into its grips the Freedom of Information Act, and informing the public about everything. It will enable the people to utilize their constitutional rights in removing dishonest people from power. This giant, corruption, is everybody's business; with the establishment of a database system, perpetrators will be easily caught and punished. In fighting, and getting rid of corruption, the media must stand as a force to grapple with. It must provide all information to the public.

"Ladies and gentlemen, this proposal, if you accept it, the country will move forward. However, if you reject it, posterity will judge you. This plan is not a masterpiece to make the crooks, or anyone happy, but for a better Liberia.

"Finally, Liberia and Liberians learn to cheerfully share

with their neighbors. If you don't share with each other or your neighbor, you will continually blur the Lone, but shining, Star. And if you got a little respect, don't give it to any other person, but to the dead. Respect the dead, and always clean their resting places. You will someday die, and disrespecting your resting area is evil. It must be punishable by law, if anyone who disrespect the dead and is caught. A thirty year prison sentence, without bill, is necessary. This is your direction and freedom. Thank You!!!!!"

Zulu Menya put all papers into a folder, and give it to the Sargent at Arm for onward submission. He looked up at the audience; there were movements and murmuring.

'Will they accept these arguments?' he thought.

CONNECT

Readers of this book are encouraged to contact
Mr. Seton with comments:
Email: shanitakseton@gmail.com

Visit author's Facebook page:
www.facebook.com/shanitakseton

Visit author's personal website:
www.shedrickseton.villagetales.com

Other GoodReads from Village Tales Publishing

By Ophelia S. Lewis
Dead Gods HM2
Heart Men (a novel)
Montserrado Stories
A Is For Africa (Children's Book)
Good Manner Alphebets (Children's Book)
My Dear Liberia (Recollections)
Journeys (a Collection of Poems)
The Dowry of Virgins (and Other Stories)
Liberia Unscrabbled (a puzzle game book)
I'm About To (Children's Book)
Where In The World Is Liberia (Children's Puzzle Book)

By Augustine B. Sherman
War of Morality

By Frank Olivier Houngnikpo
Message To God

By Augustus Y. Voahn
Uncle Jallah Will Fix It (Children's Book)

All Village Tales Publishing titles, imprints and distributed lines are available at special quanity discounts for bulk purchase for sales promotions, premiums, fundraising, educational or institutional use. For information, please visit our website;
www.villagetalespublishing.com

Join our mailing list for updates on new releases, deals, bonus content, and other great books from Village Tales Publishing.

Email Us:
villagetalespub@gmail.com
info@villagetalespublishing.com

∗ ∗ ∗ ∗

Like Us on Facebook
www.facebook.com/villagetalespublishing

∗ ∗ ∗ ∗

Village Tales Publishing provids traditional publishing services and turnkey services to individuals that seek to successfully self-publish and promote their books. We handle all aspects of publishing; editing, cover design, production, marketing and order fulfillment.

Please visit our websites:
www.villagetalespublishing.com
www.oass.villagetalespublishing.com

www.ingramcontent.com/pod-product-compliance
Lightning Source LLC
Chambersburg PA
CBHW072151170626
46813CB00004BA/1755